I0525846

Rutherford Jones

in Trouble Times Three

AIRSHIP 27 PRODUCTIONS

Rutherford Jones in Trouble Times Three

"The Mystery of Basehart Mine"; "The Stolen Script"; and "Expansion" © 2016 Robert Ricci

Published by Airship 27 Productions
www.airship27.com
www.airship27hangar.com

Interior illustrations © 2016 Andrew Ritchie
Cover illustration © 2016 Pat Carbajal

Editor: Ron Fortier
Associate Editor: Steve Bennett
Marketing and Promotions Manager: Michael Vance
Production and design by Rob Davis

All rights reserved under International and Pan-American Copyright Conventions. No part of this book may be reproduced in any manner without permission in writing from the copyright holder, except by a reviewer, who may quote brief passages in a review.

ISBN-13: 978-0692667545 (Airship 27)

ISBN-10: 0692667547

Printed in the United States of America

10 9 8 7 6 5 4 3 2 1

Table of Contents

the
MYSTERY
of
BASEHART
MINE

The dark clad figure slammed his gloved hand through the window pane and quickly turned the doorknob. Without hesitation, he flicked on the office lights. He wasn't expecting company.

"Welcome, Mr. Rutherford Jones," spoke an elderly Chinese man. "You should have knocked. That glass pane was expensive." The voice belonged to Wu Chiong, notorious gangster and leader of Oakland's vicious Nine Blades crime organization.

Jones started to reach for his rod when he felt cold steel pressed against the back of his neck.

"Please, Mr. Jones, dispel any notions of escape, my man Fong has an itchy trigger finger."

Jones raised his hands slowly. "Ok, you caught me Chiong and I told you before, I prefer being called Ford."

Wu Chiong released a hearty laugh. "Imagine, for two weeks now you've been prowling around here pretending to be a derelict digging through our trash for scraps of food. Did you really think I was stupid? Just look at you."

Rutherford Jones stood tall at over six feet, and he weighed close to two hundred pounds. In retrospect, disguising himself as a beggar wasn't one of his brightest ideas. The burly dark skinned man laughed and shrugged his shoulders. "What now, Chiong?"

The decrepit man slowly rose from his chair. He was robed in satin; an effect he thought made him look noble. Ford felt he looked pathetic.

"You're going to tell me who hired you to spy on me," demanded Chiong, waving a sharpened fingernail.

Ford grimaced. "I can't do that Wu. Besides, you'll kill me anyway."

The old man nodded. "True enough. The Nine Blades cannot appear to show weakness and no one will miss you."

Sadly enough, that was true, Ford thought. A moment of inspiration hit him.

"You wouldn't begrudge a man his last wish would you?" He didn't wait for the answer, pulling a flask from his hip pocket. "One last drink before you send me off to the next world?"

Wu hesitated, but Fong didn't. The towering Oriental ripped the flask from Ford's outstretched hands.

"Hey what gives?" Ford protested.

Fong spun the cap off with exaggerated fury. "You deserve nothing." He spat. The cruel thug tilted the flask to his lips and drank a greedy mouthful, the excess spilling down his chin.

"That was harsh." Ford said gently.

Wu Chiong had seen enough of the theatrics. "Last chance, Mr. Jones. Tell me who sent you."

Ford hesitated, running a hand over his mouth. "You sure I can't have that drink?"

In answer, Fong flipped the flask over and spilled its contents on the office floor. He sneered and tossed the empty flask back at Ford.

"Enough of this foolishness!" bellowed Wu Chiong. "Kill this man right now!"

Fong lifted his revolver slowly, intent on blowing Ford's brains out. Just as he reached hip level, he began to stagger and wipe at his eyes.

"Kill him Fong!" ordered Chiong.

Fong wanted to obey his master, but he couldn't. The flask had been filled with arsenic-laced booze. The fast killing poison was spreading rapidly through his bloodstream.

"I don't feel …" Fong began, but he never finished the statement. He was dead before his body toppled to the floor.

Instantly, Rutherford Jones scooped up the dead man's gun and spun on Wu Chiong.

"What happened?" whispered the elderly Chinese man.

Ford pointed at the empty flask. "Poison."

"But you asked to drink it?" mumbled Chiong in a state of confusion.

Again Ford laughed. "Fong and I have a history. I gambled that the selfish son of a bitch would deny my last request and gulp that crap himself. Guess my instincts were right."

Chiong was trembling now. He fell back into the chair, seeming to shrink away. "What happens to me? If you kill me the Nine Blades will stop at nothing to track you down."

Ford flipped it over in his mind. "Most likely for sure. Tell you what, you give me what I came looking for and I spare your life. Then I walk."

Wu Chiong sat up straight. "Keep talking Mr. Rutherford Jones."

"I said call me Ford. Anyway, for the last two weeks I've been stumbling around Chinatown, stinking of my own filth, in search of some bonds that I was hired to locate. Seems some of you nice fellas lifted them from a safe over in San Francisco a few months back and the owner would really appreciate their return."

Chiong smiled. "I am an honest businessman. Perhaps, one of my overzealous employees purchased some wayward bonds that had been obtained illegally. Surely it would be noble of me to return them to the rightful owner."

Ford grinned. "You keep talking now."

Chiong continued, "It appears Mr. Fong was behind this entire incident. If word were to spread that he was punished for his actions, I would maintain my stronghold on the Bay area while keeping the reputation of the Nine Blades intact." He stood up and pointed a crooked finger at Ford. "This would allow me to let you live."

Ford let out a breath of air. He had no desire to have a bounty on his head. "Works for me."

"Very well, Rutherford Jones. I will hand over the bonds to you."

Ford bent to retrieve his flask. He was shocked to find Wu Chiong in front of him when he stood up. Apparently, the old man was a lot more spry than he appeared. Chiong gripped his arm harshly. Ford gulped nervously.

"One more thing, Mr. Jones."

Ford hesitated. "What would that be?"

"I never want to see you in Chinatown ever again!"

Ford snapped his fingers, pretending frustration. "Damn, and I was just learning to appreciate your dumplings."

Wu Chiong sprinted to the door. "Kindly exit my domain."

Ford was going to answer sarcastically but thought better. With a man like, Wu Chiong, it was wiser to let him have the last say. "And the bonds?"

"You already have them." Wu gently shoved him out the door. "Check your pocket."

Stunned, Ford felt the packet in his hip pocket. Chiong must have planted it when he grabbed him. Before he could say anything, the old man slammed the door in his face.

An hour later, Rutherford Jones ascended the staircase to a second floor office in downtown Oakland. The stenciled door read - - Rutherford Jones Investigations. He knocked once and entered.

It was a tiny office; the reception area consisted of two unmatched chairs and a coat rack. This led to an inner office that was equally sparse. It had a worn desk with a broken table lamp and a rolling chair. In front of it was a cheap wooden chair. Both chairs were occupied.

Behind the desk sat a scrawny man in his late twenties. The youth looked sallow and the wool suit he wore was too large for his frame and too warm for the weather. The nameplate in front of him read: Rutherford Jones.

"You're late Rufus!" The thin man barked at Ford as he entered.

Ford didn't make eye contact. He mumbled, "Sorry, Mr. Jones. I delivered those papers from Chinee town likes you asked." He deliberately mispronounced his words.

The frail looking man behind the desk shook his head in a defeated manner. "See what I have to work with?" he asked the man seated across from him.

The other fellow was a complete contrast to the skinny man. He was a broad shouldered, good looking chap, neatly dressed in a pinstripe suit. He began to say something when the thin man interjected.

"Rufus, I don't know what I'm going to do with you! Mr. Ellis here came all the way from Redding to seek my services and you just barge in here like an ox hurtling out of the corral."

Ford continued to keep his eyes downcast. "So sorry Mr. Jones, but if I don't do my mop work now I'll miss my ride home."

"That would serve you right," answered the thin man, yanking on the knot of his tie. He turned to his client, Peter Ellis. "If you don't object, I'll let this man continue his cleaning while we talk." He winked at Ellis. "Man's not too bright anyway. I'm surprised he can put one foot in front of the other."

Peter Ellis cleared his throat. He glanced at Ford nervously, but the big black man didn't make eye contact. "I guess that would be okay, Mr. Jones."

The skinny man wiped a hand across his lips. "I'm parched. Mind if I indulge?" He asked holding up an expensive bottle of scotch. Ellis waved at him nonchalantly, but Ford cleared his throat loudly.

The booze had been won in a card game down on the waterfront against

Mickey 'Humpback' Dolan. Ford was saving it for a special occasion.

Seeing the anger on Ford's face, the pale skinned man skipped a glass and took a healthy chug. "Now where were we, Mr. Ellis?"

Angered about the scotch, Ford sauntered over to the wash bucket and lifted the mop. The bucket had already been filled by the skinny man.

Peter Ellis pulled out a map from his breast pocket. He laid it out on the desk and pointed at a large area he had circled on it. "This is Basehart Mining Company out in Redding." He tapped at a portion of Northern California on the map.

The skinny man prompted him. "This is the mine you came to see me about?"

"Yes, Mr. Jones. You see my grandfather willed this to me a year or so back. Told me I'd be set for life from the ore being mined there. Only, things haven't worked out like that."

"Go on." The thin man ordered.

Peter Ellis pointed at the map. "Most of the gold mines in California have dried up, but my grandfather assured me this one had many untapped silver veins, enough to keep going another twenty years."

Ford splashed water on the floor, swishing his mop back and forth while listening intently.

"My lawyer, Marion Preston, informs me that the mine is dried up and that I should sell the equipment and get rid of the land. Only, I can't believe him, Mr. Jones. My grandfather was adamant that this vein was prosperous."

The thin man reached into the desk drawer again, retrieving the bottle of scotch. He let an eye drift casually at Ford before pouring himself a healthy dose. "So why not get a second opinion? Why come to a private dick for help?"

Ellis wiped a bead of sweat from his forehead. His teeth began to chatter. "That's the rub. I did hire a team of state inspectors to examine Basehart."

"And what did they discover?"

"I don't know."

Ford stopped mopping. The skinny man put his glass down.

"They never returned," Peter Ellis concluded.

The thin man knocked back his drink and returned the bottle to its drawer. He had put a healthy dent in it.

"Are you going to take my case?" Ellis asked anxiously.

The thin man put both hands on the desk, pretending to ponder the situation. Ford pulled his mop from the bucket and tapped the wooden end once on the floor.

"Yes. I will agree to investigate."

Ellis sighed with relief. "Thank goodness."

The thin man shook his hand. "I charge twenty dollars a day plus travel expenses." He pointed at Ford. "Rufus, here, moonlights as my driver and muscle. I'd like to have him investigate firsthand. I think you should arrange to get him on as a hired hand."

Peter Ellis nodded enthusiastically. "He'll be perfect for excavation. Big negro like him will be appreciated." He stared at Ford. "Are you sure about this? You said he wasn't too bright."

The skinny man came around the desk and gave Ford a hearty slap on the back. "Rufus knows his place. Just point the big lug in the right direction, and he'll do his part. Just make sure he don't get no alcohol in him. The man's a wreck, can't handle his liquor worth a match."

Rutherford Jones returned his mop to the bucket. He finally raised his eyes to Peter Ellis. "I know my place."

Ellis felt a chill go down his spine. He imagined the muscular fellow getting angry at someone. The image wasn't pretty. "Then it's settled."

The skinny man ushered him to the door. "I'll be in touch tonight to iron out the details. Rest assured, Mr. Ellis, if something is afoul, Rutherford Jones will uncover it."

•   •   •

After walking Peter Ellis down the staircase, the skinny man returned to the office to find Ford Jones waiting, a stern look on his face.

"He knows his place?" Ford muttered. "What I know is you owe me a bottle of hooch, Jimmy."

Jimmy was the thin man's actual name, except, no one ever called him that. Everyone referred to him by his nickname, Bottles. Jimmy 'Bottles' McGee was an alcoholic. He was also the face of Rutherford Jones Investigations.

"C'mon Ford, don't begrudge me a couple of snoots of the good stuff. Didn't I just collar you a big job?"

Ford sighed in acknowledgment. "You did Jimmy, but man, that scotch was hard to come by. You're probably half off the shelf already and didn't even taste it."

Bottles shook his head in protest. "Nah, that was my first one today. Swear on my sweet old Aunt Petunia."

Ford laughed. "You ain't got no Aunt Petunia, Jimmy. But you did good." He took the bottle from his desk and tossed it to the skinny boy. Bottles cradled it like someone had tossed an infant to him.

"Easy, Ford! My reflexes ain't been right in this salty air!"

Jimmy 'Bottles' McGee had been playing this role for the last year successfully. He would lure the clients in, unaware that the actual boss was a black man. It was a necessary deception in these tough times.

"You're going to have to lay off the rotgut for a couple of days while I'm up in Redding. I can't have a situation like last month."

The situation Ford was referring to was an awkward moment where Jimmy had emerged naked except for his socks and neck tie, and singing off-key Irish ballads in downtown Oakland before the local PD had allowed him to sleep it off in one of their free suites. Ford had lost his investigators license for two weeks over that incident.

Bottles McGee stared at the scotch before returning it to the desk drawer. "I can behave for a couple of days, Ford. Besides, with the money we'll make on this caper, I can afford to have Linda Mae fry me up a big old slab of beef."

Linda Mae was the first-floor tenant. She ran a second-hand jewelry store. Both the jewelry and Linda Mae had seen better days. Over the last five weeks or so, Jimmy and Linda Mae had found comfort in commiserating each other's woes over cheap booze served in dirty coffee cups.

Linda Mae knew Jimmy wasn't Rutherford Jones. She wasn't privy to the fact that Rufus, the hired hand, was in actuality Rutherford Jones. Both men felt it was wiser to leave well enough alone.

Jimmy locked the desk drawer and handed Ford the key. Ford knew it was strictly symbolic, but he appreciated the gesture.

"She's a good girl Jimmy, and still young enough to whip out a few young ones. Why don't you dwell on that while I'm gone?"

Bottles McGee snorted. "It ain't like that Ford. Why we haven't even kissed yet."

Ford slapped a beefy arm around the tiny man. "You know you might find those lips have a better use than knocking back booze. Just promise me you'll think about it?"

Jimmy nodded positively. He listened to Ford's advice. They had met a couple of years back, when Ford was tossed out of a saloon that catered to a whites-only mentality. Jimmy had been tossed out as well for his drunken buffoonery and the two men had bonded that day over a cheap bottle in a back alley in Oakland. Neither man had ever questioned the other's position, instead they had learned to play off each other's strengths and the results had been the creation of Rutherford Jones Investigations.

The façade had led to many playful encounters like today, where Jimmy would overplay his role. In fact, he was gracious to Ford for taking him in as a partner. Likewise, Ford valued Jimmy's loyalty. They had a good racket going.

"If I'm going to have to get out of Oakland for a couple of days, I want to see Myra." Ford announced to no one in particular. When Jimmy didn't respond, he commented, "Do you think she's still mad at me?"

Bottles McGee whistled loudly. "What do you think big guy? Would you forgive someone who got you fired?"

Myra Ellington was a sultry siren. Her jazz vocals had transformed her into an overnight sensation in San Francisco. The cocoa-skinned beauty had been on the verge of a national breakout until Rutherford Jones had stepped into her life. He hadn't planned on it, but Ford had thrust her into one of his investigations while she was the headliner at the Ivory Keys piano bar. Ford had been casing the joint for weeks, trying to get the backdrop on the owner who was shortchanging his East Coast financiers. During his research, Ford had fallen in love with Myra Ellington, but all that ended when he busted her mobster boss. Myra went from having her own dressing room with champagne service to singing as a cocktail waitress in a questionable gentlemen's establishment in one of the seedier parts of Oakland that catered to hard-up miners and drifters looking for action. She hadn't returned any of Ford's messages for weeks.

"I don't know Jimmy, but I gotta try."

Bottles McGee nodded his approval. "I think she might come around big guy. Your charm will work on her."

• • •

Downtown Oakland was a vast difference from glitzy Los Angeles or artistic San Francisco. The nightlife was just an extension of the daytime struggle to get a better place in life. Myra Ellington was employed at the Pinebluff Parrot. Employed was a joke. More appropriately, detained was the verb that described her relationship with the underground gentlemen's club. The joint floated under the radar of the authorities in part mostly because many of the attendees were off duty law enforcement officers and lower seeded politicians looking for cheap thrills. The dancers were topless except for their pasties and the drinks were watered down. There was an adjacent lounge to enjoy live music, an excuse for men to validate their presence at the club. It was in the lounge that Ford spotted Myra.

She was as beautiful as ever, her coffee colored skin poured into a dress tight enough to show off all her curves, yet classy enough to elevate her above the cheesy surroundings. She was halfway through a ballad when a drunken sailor got a little feisty. Before the bouncer could intervene, Myra launched a vicious kick to the man's midsection. He landed on his rear before being dragged away by a towering bald man wearing leather gloves which covered his hidden brass knuckles.

Ford grabbed a beer at the bar, but after noticing the grime around the rim didn't drink it. He waited until Myra had finished her song before clapping wildly along with the spirited crowd.

"Myra, it's me, Ford!"

The voluptuous woman turned to him and a sly grin spread over her face. Her breasts strained against the dress as she shimmied over to him.

"Rutherford B. Jones!" She declared.

She then proceeded to slap him as hard as she could across the face.

Stung, Ford clutched at his cheek. "Why did you do that baby?"

She slapped him again. "I'm not your baby!" She started to raise her hand again, but, this time, Ford caught her wrist. He was gentle, but firm.

"Okay, maybe I deserved that," he admitted, "but enough is enough!"

At that moment, the gigantic bouncer appeared. The lights from the club beamed off his shaven head. "This guy giving you a hard time?" He barked; his eyes locked on Ford.

Ford didn't back away. "Just having a conversation with the lady, friend."

Before Myra could confirm, the bouncer had an iron grip on Ford's shoulder. "I ain't your friend." He swung a looping right at Ford, but he was expecting it. Ford blocked the blow with his left forearm and shoved at the bouncer's chest, knocking him into a group of lively sailors. The officers took offense at their beer being spilled.

"What gives?" Howled one of them.

Before he could say anything further, the man's mouth ate a fistful of brass knuckles from the bouncer. Blood and teeth spewed on his comrades' uniforms.

"That ain't right," noted Ford. Before he could join the fracas, he saw Myra shatter a beer mug up against the bouncer's head.

"He had it coming," she said defiantly. "Hitting one of our enlisted boys."

The giant bouncer wobbled a couple of times before the wounded sailor was able to deliver a knockout blow. The crowd began to surge toward the action. Unfortunately, so did additional bouncers. Ford felt someone get him in a bear hug; the arms gripped him like a vice. Calmly, he rammed his head backward, striking his attacker in the face, breaking the man's nose.

"Oh God! You just hit the owner's nephew!" cried Myra. "I was just getting use to this dive!"

Ford smiled. His blood was churning. He rifled a fist into an onrushing bouncer. The sailors swarmed the man like a pack of wolves, downing their prey in seconds.

The sound of sirens filled the air as police cars careened their way to the Parrot. Ford didn't hesitate. He heaved Myra over his shoulder like a sack of potatoes and sprinted for the kitchen. He was able to exit into a back alley before the Oakland Police shouldered their way into the lounge. The Mayor had warned the owners that shenanigans would no longer be tolerated, and he kept his word. Uniformed and undercover vice operations stormed the club, destroying the alcohol and breaking every piece of glass they could find.

Fortunately, Ford Jones and Myra Ellington were well out of range by then. Myra had lost a shoe during the exodus.

"Rutherford Jones, you unsavory clam! I hate you!" she snarled.

He couldn't help but laugh. He hadn't had this much fun since the incident in San Francisco. "I know baby."

She snapped at his back. "I'm not your baby."

He felt the softness of her skin beneath the dress. It felt like a dream, one he had missed. He plopped her on her feet. She yelped as one bare foot hit the rough pavement.

"You know I can't go back there," she stated.

Ford kissed her roughly. She didn't resist.

"You don't want to."

She hugged him tightly. "No, I don't"

• • •

An hour later they strolled back to the office building arm in arm. Bottles McGee was sitting on the stoop. He was eating sponge cake with Linda Mae. Linda Mae smiled at Ford.

"Good evening Rufus. I see you have company."

Myra stared at the worn down woman curiously. "What did she call you?"

Ford placed a hand over her mouth and ushered her up the stairs, much to Linda Mae's dismay.

"Did you see that Jimmy?" The girl asked incredulously. "The girl didn't even know Rufus' name and she went upstairs with him! Honestly, some of those people make me wonder."

Jimmy smiled. He knew very well that Myra knew Ford's name. The burly investigator would have to clue his beau in on their ruse before encountering Linda Mae again. He fed her a spoonful of cake. "You're wonderful in the kitchen, Linda Mae."

The woman snorted. She had downed a few drinks earlier in the evening. Jimmy had graciously declined. "More for me," she had joked. "It's beautiful out here Jimmy."

Bottles McGee slid an arm around her waist. Maybe Ford was right. Maybe Linda Mae was the one. He summoned his courage. "Linda Mae, there is something I'd like to ask you."

"Yes, Jimmy?"

He tugged at his tie. The collar of his shirt seemed tighter, and he wondered if he could get the words out.

"Spit it out, Jimmy."

Bottles McGee swallowed. Here it goes, he thought. "Linda Mae would you like to go inside with me?" He stared at her as if his life depended on it.

"Sure I would."

"You would?"

Linda Mae nodded. "Yeah, I been craving a drink all night. Let's go have one before I get too tired."

Jimmy's shoulders dropped, the air releasing from his lungs. He slumped forward, retrieving the plate of sponge cake. "Sure, why not?"

He watched as Linda Mae staggered up the short stairs to her apartment, her tipsy movements alerting him to the fact that the coffee refills she had been sneaking inside to have probably contained something stronger than cream and sugar. His ears detected rough sounds from the office above. Ford and Myra were getting reacquainted.

"Looks like I'll be sacking out on your sofa tonight." He yelled ahead to Linda Mae. When she didn't answer, he hustled his movements a bit faster and found her at the kitchen table. Her loud snoring informed him that she was out for the night. He thought about carrying her to the bedroom, gave up on the idea, and threw a comforter over her instead.

He listened quietly to the moaning coming from above before he then grabbed a spot on the sofa and covered his ears with a pillow.

• • •

Rutherford Jones woke up happy. He felt the warm body of Myra Ellington curled up beside him. They were reclining on a fold out cot that he kept in the broom closet. Bottles McGee possessed a matching unit. Times were tough and the two men felt it made sense to use their office as a residence.

"You smell good," he whispered as Myra began to stir.

The sultry siren gave out a sleepy yawn before bolting upright. The thin sheet covering her breasts fell away for a moment allowing Ford a reminder of how fortunate he had been.

Myra clutched the sheets fiercely. "Seriously? That wasn't a nightmare last night?"

Ford smiled and kissed her cheek. "Don't give me that tone. You weren't drunk and no one forced you to come back with me."

She jumped out of bed, wrapping the bedsheet around her. Ford was naked except for his boxers. He didn't make any move to cover up.

Myra picked up her dress off the office desk. It was covered with remnants from the previous night's battle. She smelled beer and could see bloodstains on it.

"Ruined!" She barked at Ford. "I just bought that for my act." She tossed the dress to the floor defiantly. "I guess it doesn't matter. After your big tilt, I won't be welcomed back at the Parrot."

Ford walked over and hugged her. He could feel her soft curves through the thin sheet. "Baby, you don't need that place. You're better than that."

He opened the broom closet and fished through one of his duffel bags. He came across a long sleeved button down shirt that he kept for special occasions. He sniffed it, satisfied that it would pass muster, and tossed it over to her. "Put this on. I'll have Bottles fetch something from Linda Mae for you to wear."

A crease burrowed on Myra's face. "Linda Mae, the white lady downstairs? I don't think she's too fond of me. Did you see the cock-eyed look she threw at me?"

Ford laughed. "Yes, I did. In fact, I see that every night. She's a drunk, Myra, a harmless drunk. Besides, she's a good neighbor, and I think Jimmy has the hots for her."

Myra signaled for him to turn around as she dropped the sheet and donned his shirt. Ford itched to peek, but thought better of it.

"If you vouch for her, I'll deal with it," she decided. She left the top two buttons undone, her breasts swollen against the material.

Ford gulped. He suddenly felt thirsty. He gave her an arched eyebrow.

Myra shook her head negatively. "Whatever you're about to suggest, just can it. I had a moment of weakness last night. As soon as I borrow some clothes from your fruity neighbor, I'm going to blow this place."

She put her hands on her hips, expecting him to protest.

"Probably a good idea," Ford countered. "Bottles dug up some work yesterday, and that's why I headed downtown to see you."

The beautiful woman hid her disappointment. "Why tell me? We aren't exactly a couple."

"Myra, you know how I feel about you. I'd do anything for you, but you're right about us. You have a career and goals. I'm just a guy trying to make it as a private dick, and I even have to use Jimmy as a cover because people don't want to trust a black man."

"You don't need to preach to me, Ford. I'm not even welcome in the clubs that pay me to perform. I feel like an attraction at the zoo."

Ford tugged on a pair of work pants and a cutoff shirt that emphasized his muscular frame. He opened the window to let in some air.

"I don't smell eggs and bacon." He noted. "Maybe Bottles finally got lucky. Either that or they really tied one on."

Myra crinkled her nose. "And that's another thing, Rutherford Jones. Why in the world did that floozy call you Rufus?"

Ford laughed. "When Bottles and I concocted the scam to switch identities I knew better than to give myself a name like Jimmy McGee. Rufus was my father's name."

"I didn't know that." She looked surprised. "So why aren't you named Rufus?"

The big man grabbed his socks and shoes. "I was named after President Rutherford B. Hayes."

Myra smiled. "Most colored men named after presidents go by Lincoln. Why Hayes?"

Ford grinned, recalling his mother's recitation of the story. "It's a long story, but I'll try to make it short. Yes, Lincoln got the boat in the water, but Hayes played a big part too. If it weren't for him, the country might not know about W.E.B. Du Bois."

Myra nodded. "I'm aware of the Slater Fund. My grandfather was one of the first blacks to win that scholarship because of President Hayes. I can see why your family would name you after him."

Ford turned away from the window. "It was more than that. You see, during the battle of Fox's Gap, there was a frightened young black man trapped under a heap of dead bodies during the Battle of South Mountain. That man was John Jacobs, my grandfather.

"John had been abandoned by his troops and felt his days on Mother Earth were over. He was just about to give up when Lt. Col Rutherford B. Hayes and the 23rd Ohio Infantry rushed in to save him. Mr. Hayes suffered a grievous wound that day, but he saved my grandfather during that battle. Grandpa never forgot. He reminded my momma every day of her childhood that not all white folks were selfish. She repaid the Lord by naming me after her daddy's savior."

"That's quite a story, a black man with a white President's name." Myra fussed. "Too bad, we'll never see no black man become President."

Ford shrugged nonchalantly. "I won't agree with that. I believe that's a possibility someday."

Myra kissed him gently. "Ford Jones, optimist, I knew there was a reason I let you hang around." She wafted a hand beneath her nose. "I smell bacon. Why don't you downstairs and round us up some?"

Ford studied her hips as she turned. "Sounds good, and I better hustle you up some clothes while I'm at it."

•　•　•

Jimmy McGee sat patiently at the kitchen table, spooning heapfuls of sugar into his coffee cup. He still wore the crumpled up suit from yesterday. It appeared to hang off him even more this morning.

"This bacon is burned!" Ford protested, spitting out a chunk into the sink.

"I was on my own," Jimmy explained. He directed a thumb over to the sofa. Linda Mae was sprawled out, covered up in a heavy bathrobe despite the heat. Her snoring was loud and throaty. She'd be out for awhile. "Sleeping beauty missed my bugle call."

"You devil! You tired the poor woman out!"

Jimmy shrugged. "Yeah, but not the way your filthy mind is thinking." He pointed to a manila envelope on the table. "I counted the bonds. There's a lot more money than those insurance guys mentioned."

The insurance guys were the client who had hired Ford to recover the bonds. A claim had been put on them, but it had trickled down through the grapevine that Wu Chiong had purchased the stolen bonds. The insurance company had held up payment until Ford had confirmed their suspicions.

"What are you driving at Bottles?" Ford inquired.

Jimmy shrugged again, stirring his spoon slowly. "Just thinking out loud friend. Those insurance guys are not hurting for money, and they would have to be pay off the claim anyway, so what if…"

"Skip it!" Ford interrupted. "That's blood money, Jimmy. The Nine Blades iced a butler and a delivery boy during that robbery. I don't want that on my conscience."

Jimmy squinted. "Still, it's tempting."

Ford opened the icebox and pulled out some fresh bacon. He couldn't subject Myra to the swill Jimmy had rousted up.

"Bottles, I need you to drop those bonds off… all of them. I also need you to come up with an excuse to keep Myra here for a couple of days."

Jimmy dropped the spoon, letting a little of the coffee splash on his wrist. Fortunately, it was already cold.

"She's staying here? With me? Myra? Beautiful, curvy Myra?" He shook his head. "Wouldn't be proper. Besides, our place ain't right for a dish like Myra. We don't even have a bath tub!"

"Who said anything about our place?" Ford protested. He gestured around at the apartment. "I was thinking Linda Mae might appreciate some company. You know—female company. It would be good for both of them."

This time, Jimmy banged the spoon on purpose. He was about to shout when Linda Mae rolled over on the sofa, emitting a low moan, the tell-tale sign of a hangover.

"Coffee!" The woman pleaded.

Jimmy bolted from his seat and poured her a cup of the lukewarm brew. He didn't bother with cream or sugar.

"Here you go kid. This will help out."

She took the mug and guzzled a mouthful. "It's terrible, but thank you Jimmy." She pinched his cheek. "My sweet Jimmy. What would I do without you?"

Probably drink yourself to death, Ford thought.

"I've got the cure for that coming up." He hollered.

Linda Mae shook the cobwebs out of her head. "Rufus? Here in my apartment? But, I'm not decent!"

No, you might never be, Ford thought.

Jimmy took the mug away and went to get her a refill. He elbowed Ford on the way to the counter.

"What did you do with the hooker, Rufus? That doesn't go over well in this part of town."

Ford turned and stared incredulously at the woman. He was about to say something rude when Jimmy elbowed his way past him again.

"Second round my lady." The skinny youth declared, eager to change the subject.

Linda Mae forced down another gulpful before making a grimace of pain. "What the hell did you lace that with Jimmy?"

He feigned ignorance before admitting, "I dropped a couple of aspirin in there Linda Mae. Just trying to be helpful."

Ford pulled a few strips of bacon from the frying pan and tossed them on a plate.

"This will soak up the booze."

Linda Mae snatched up the bacon, holding her nose. "The smell is making me nauseous."

The bags under eyes were chestnut size. Ford wondered when the woman had last slept a full night. He was beginning to question his proposal when she turned to him again.

"Rufus, you didn't answer me. Where's the hooker?"

A shadow entered the kitchen. It was Myra. The angry look on her face informed Ford that she had heard the woman's accusations.

Linda Mae gasped.

"She's naked!"

Myra arched an eyebrow, tugging at the borrowed shirt she wore. She swiveled her hips deliberately as she shimmied over to the counter top. Whistling, she calmly poured a cup of coffee.

"Good morning Miss Myra," Jimmy said in a monotone voice.

Myra gave Jimmy a fake smile. "Is it now?"

Linda Mae struggled to get off the sofa. On the second attempt, she made it. She dragged herself over to a closet and yanked a bathrobe off a hanger.

"Please young lady, I don't know what type of upbringing you came from, but we don't parade around like that!"

Myra begrudgingly accepted the robe. She slipped it over Ford's shirt.

"If I could just borrow one of your dresses, I'll be on my way."

No one said anything.

"I'll bring it back of course." She followed up.

Linda Mae seemed disgusted. "You poor woman. Don't tell me this brute dragged you here and threw you out? Shame on you Rufus! And to think my Jimmy employs you."

Jimmy made an awkward face. He turned to Ford for help.

"I have work today," Ford stated to no one in particular.

Myra sighed and threw her hands up. "This is ridiculous!"

"The smell is making me nauseous."

Linda Mae was starting to stabilize. "Yes, it is." She poked an angry finger at Jimmy. "You're the role model here. Show your guy how it's done. Show him how to treat a lady."

Jimmy 'Bottles' McGee cleared his throat, wishing beyond all hope that he had spiked his own coffee this morning. He stood erect as he addressed Ford.

"Rufus, this behavior is unacceptable. Linda Mae is correct. You have been cruel to this poor innocent girl. I demand you make it right!" He turned to Myra and held her hands. "You deserve that."

Linda Mae grabbed the other hand. Her palm was sweaty and shaking, but Myra didn't flinch.

"It's okay, really…"

"No, Jimmy is right." Linda Mae began, "Rufus needs to learn our ways. It's going to start right now. You're not going anywhere. You staying here with Jimmy and I until Rufus earns your respect."

Ford couldn't believe his stroke of fortune. He started to speak, but then thought better of it.

Jimmy McGee bought into the act full throttle. "You are a clever bird, my love. Rufus will be gone for a few days working up in Redding. I insist Miss Myra stay here as our guest until we right this wrong."

Ford chewed his bacon slowly.

"Well, Rufus, what says you to that?" Linda Mae demanded.

Ford continued to chew carefully. When he was done he wiped a hand across his mouth.

"I'm waiting!" Linda Mae pressed.

Ford turned and faced Myra. "I'm sorry."

A smug look crossed Linda Mae's face. "That's better, Rufus."

He interrupted her. "I'm sorry, but I'll be needing that shirt back before I go."

Myra growled loudly. She wasn't acting. "You're a heel!"

"That he is." Jimmy echoed.

•   •   •

Bottles McGee gripped the steering wheel tightly. He was jonesing for a drink, but it would have to wait until he dropped Ford off at Basehart Mining in Redding. They were closing in on the location.

"Are you sure you don't want to take a rod?" The skinny youth inquired.

Ford shook his head. "Too dangerous. I'm supposed to be a hired laborer. Why would I have a gun?" He didn't wait for a reply. "Did Peter Ellis mention anything else?"

"Nah, he was pretty nervous on the phone." Jimmy had dialed him up from a drugstore phone after dropping off the bonds in Downtown Oakland. "He cleared everything for you."

"Go on." Ford prodded.

"You'll be part of the development mining crew. All they do is get rid of the waste. The fancy term is excavation."

Ford had no problem with hard labor. He could use the exercise and truth be known he was excited about this case. Ever since he was a boy, he marveled at the idea of being a miner and discovering riches.

"This guy I'm working for, Bradley Jenkins, what did you dig up on him?"

"The foreman. Tough cookie. Former LAPD cop got busted by a young detective named O'Leary. They drummed him off the force, and he somehow wormed his way into Basehart."

Ford fondly recalled the case. "I've met Billy O'Leary, good guy. He's been chasing after that masked vigilante the last year or so."

Jimmy frowned. "Which one you talking about? Those guys are popping up like weeds in a garden."

Ford sighed. "This one's not a guy, Bottles. She's an angel, a long haired blonde angel."

"Yeah, I heard about that chick. They say she's a crack shot with a .22 and even more dangerous with her hands."

They passed a sign welcoming them to Redding, California. Bottles McGee slammed on the brakes and anchored the car on the side of the road.

"This is where I drop you, big guy."

Ford nodded, it was still early enough to make it before sundown. He'd try to hitch a ride, but wasn't expecting any assistance in this economy.

"Ellis says the black folks run a tight-knit unit. One of the older guys, Otis Crabtree will be your contact."

"Can I trust him?"

Bottles flipped his notes over. "Ellis informed me that Crabtree has been working there for decades. If not for his shade of skin, he'd be the foreman."

"Well, thanks for that piece of information."

"Don't shoot the messenger, Ford."

Ford relaxed. "It's okay, Jimmy. Remember what I told you. Lay off the rotgut. And for god sakes keep Linda Mae away from the bottle. You guys will never make babies if she keeps polluting her system that way!"

Jimmy turned red. "Shucks, Ford, I was ready to make the move last night but she keeled over before I could work my charm. Maybe with Myra around, Linda Mae will pick up some hints."

Ford's face soured. "Sooner or later we'll have to deal with this identity switch, Jimmy but for now, I'd prefer keeping Linda Mae in the dark. That might not be as easy with Myra around."

Jimmy pondered the situation. "I think Myra understands better than anyone why we did it."

"Yeah, you're probably right."

Jimmy handed him a jug of water. "Go easy on that. This heat isn't letting up, and you'll have to hoof it from here on."

Ford accepted the jug and grabbed his bag.

"Contact Ellis every evening. If I need to reach you I'll find a way to contact him. This guy, Otis Crabtree should be able to help out."

Jimmy turned on the ignition. "Keep on your toes around Jenkins. The whispers I listened to weren't kind."

Ford exited and closed the door of the sedan.

"I'll be fine, Jimmy."

"I know Ford." He threw the gear into drive and rolled away.

Ford cupped his hands together and yelled. "Lay off that scotch. I'll know if you add water!"

Bottles McGee acknowledged with a wave of his arm as he peeled away.

•   •   •

Rutherford Jones gazed down at his shoes. They were covered with grit. He had traveled the remaining distance to the mining camp on foot, never once spotting a car. He removed his shoes and shook out the dirt.

The excavation crew inhabited several pop-up tents at the base of the mountain. Ford glanced at a group of black men throwing dice and sipping on moonshine. He drifted over slowly.

"Who you be looking for?" one of the youths asked. He was a scrawny boy, most likely a messenger and not one of the slab movers. The boy's hand was soft when Ford shook it.

"The name is Rufus. I'm supposed to report for work with Mr. Bradley Jenkins."

An elderly man broke from the huddle. He had shocking white hair adorning his large head. Sunspots and age spots battled for real estate on it. He grinned widely, a huge gap where his front teeth had been.

"Welcome, son, we been expecting you." The man extended his hand. His grip was like a vice. The man had to have been in his seventies, but his strength was still evident. "I'm Otis Crabtree. I supervise the grunts."

Ford released his hand and tried to muster up a confused look.

"I was told to see Mr. Jenkins."

Otis slapped him on the back. "And you will friend, but don't be looking forward to it. Jenkins runs a tight ship. The only time you'll see him is when you have a problem, and problems are taken care of fast around here."

"Understood."

Otis pointed to the circle of tents. "That's our sleeping quarters. Latrines are around back. We feed you three times a day, mostly potatoes with a speck of meat. It ain't free. Basehart deducts it from your wages. You get paid once a week, on Friday.

"I hear Peter Ellis, himself, vouched for you? That's mighty high praise. And from the looks of those arms, hard work won't be a problem. I get the orders from Jenkins in the evening, and I dish out the work in the morning. That's the routine. Got it?"

Ford didn't answer.

"Good." Otis continued, "As you can see, we unwind at night. This place is off the beaten path so noise aint' a worry. There are no ladies around so it's just gambling and boozing. All I ask is that there are no beefs. The work is hard enough without having to break up battles. You fight and you're gone."

Ford had a hunch. He chanced an opportunity to intervene. "So what about the production crew? Do we get a shot at working on it? I never seen the inside of a mine before."

The old black man eyed him wearily. "Another adventurer, huh? All you boys are the same, dreaming of a pot of gold, or in this case, silver. Sorry, sonny, that part of the business is off-limits."

"How come?" Ford asked boldly.

Otis laughed so hard tears rolled down his eyes. He grabbed his belly to stop shaking.

"You are a real hoot, son. How come? Would you trust a bunch a black fellah around a pile of raw silver?"

Ford smiled sheepishly. "I see your point."

"Why don't you go grab a blanket, son. You look like that trek knocked some years off your life. You can fill that jug up in the morning. I don't recommend you drink the well water unless you want to be sitting in the latrine for a day."

"I'll take your advice, Mr. Crabtree. I'm gonna grab a few winks."

Otis turned back to his crew; none of the men acknowledged Ford. They were products of desperate times. All newcomers were greeted with suspicion and a touch of loathing.

I'm better off, Ford thought. The less they know my intentions, the more chance I have of uncovering this plot.

•   •   •

Ford woke early. He had no choice. The roar of heavy drilling startled him out of a sound sleep. He had dreamed he was lying on a beach, straining to hear the waves crash, but unable to locate the ocean. All he could see for miles was sand.

"Get moving!" A voice ordered him.

He felt a rough kick at his shin and opened his eyes to see a towering white man standing over him. The man sported a handlebar mustache and some worn chaps over his denim pants.

"We don't take kindly to loafers." The man's voice boomed in Ford's ears. "I'm Jenkins, the foreman. Mr. Ellis told me he'd found a fellow he thought could help out up here. Don't make a fool out of him."

Ford hustled out of his blankets. "No, sir. Sorry, sir."

Jenkins sneered at him. "Don't be a kiss up. I don't like your kind. I don't trust your kind. I'm committing your face to memory, right now. You get out of line, and I'll see to it your black ass never works again. Understand?"

Ford nodded. It took all his willpower to remain silent.

Satisfied that he'd get no backtalk, Jenkins hitched up his pants and wandered out of the tent. A moment later Otis Crabtree came barreling in. The old man was out of breath.

"Son of a bitch!" He cursed. "The boys told me Jenkins was on his way down from the lift. I was gonna warn you, but I ain't as spry as I once was."

"He always so friendly?"

Otis grinned his toothless smile.

"Son, you got off easy. I seen him pistol whip men on the first day just to impress the other fellows." He turned to peek out the tent. "I heard he was a lawman once. Got caught up in some foul business and now he's up here strutting around like a rooster."

"Anyone challenge him yet?"

The frail man shook his head violently. "I don't recommend it, son. There's no law around these parts and a black man hasn't got much value in Northern California. Mr. Ellis, he's been nice enough to provide us with steady work, but even he don't interfere with the evil stuff that goes on here."

"What do you mean by that?"

Otis shrugged, "Better off not said, son." He held open the tent flap. "Unless you want to be terminated on your first day, I'd suggest moving your butt up to the line."

•   •   •

The line turned out to be an efficient means of waste removal. The huge slabs of stone and dirt were removed in handcarts, later to be transported by truck to the city and sold to developers. This tiresome labor helped support the Basehart Mining Company until a vein was struck.

Ford grunted his way through a few hours of heavy lifting, happy for the exercise. The sun wasn't too strong today, and the strain felt good on his muscles.

The other men didn't approach him. They all worked in tandem, lifting and sorting stones on to the carts. Otis wandered back and forth, sometimes giving directions, but mostly recording numbers on a sheet with his pencil. Occasionally, he ladled out water to the men so that they wouldn't get dehydrated.

"How come no one is talking to me?" Ford asked, when the old timer offered him a drink.

Otis shrugged. "Just the way it is. Look at you. You look like a brick. Someone's been feeding you. That means you've been working. And if you been working, it means you got some smarts. The boys fear that. They worry about losing this job every day."

"Mr. Ellis told me the company is not producing a lot of silver."

"Oh, he did, did he?"

"That's right."

Otis dropped the ladle in the water bucket. "Now why would a big shot businessman like Peter Ellis be sharing company secrets with you?"

Ford got nervous. He knew he had to venture an explanation.

"He told me I could trust you, Otis. Said you've been working here ever since his grandfather opened the place."

Otis nodded. "That's true. Old man Ellis and I shared a lot of long evenings. Those were glorious days. You'd hear the blasting and then all of a sudden it would get real quiet before the whooping began. Oh how I miss that noise!"

"You're talking about a silver strike?"

"Damn right I am! Old Basehart was farting out ore filled with silver."

Ford hesitated but then decided to ask. "And now?"

Otis shook his head sadly. "Now they say she's dried up."

"But you don't believe it?"

The old man rubbed a dirty hand across his chin. "Not for a second. These mines are like a woman. They bleed heavy for years before the flow halts, but this one ain't ready for the pasture yet. I'm telling you the old girl's got some life in her yet."

"So what do you think is happening?"

Otis glanced around in both directions. He made sure none of the laborers were in earshot.

"I think Bradley Jenkins might be short changing the boss. Of course, I can't prove it. The development and production sides of the business are separated. I have no access to what's being pulled out of the long hole."

Ford gambled. "Anyone you know up at that camp?"

"Nope. Jenkins fired all the old crew. Replaced them with his city slicker friends. Told Mr. Ellis they had the proper credentials. I highly doubt that."

"Don't the state come by and regulate the mining?"

Otis slapped his knee. "Ain't you been listening to anything? The law don't exists up here. Jenkins buys them off and those he can't purchase, he uses other means of persuasion."

"What kind of means?"

"The kind which don't leave your kin no parts to bury."

•   •   •

The rest of the day went without incident. Ford stopped counting after he had carted off over twenty loads of stone. His hands were raw and aching, but he didn't let it stop him from letting off some steam.

He spent a good twenty minutes tossing stones at a circle he had notched off on a low part of the mountainside. He kept track of how many times his toss landed inside the circle. He was up to fourteen.

"Where did you learn to throw like that?" A voice asked.

It was the young man who had greeted him upon entering camp yesterday. His name was Samson, but he preferred to be called Sammy. Probably a good call. This Samson weighed less than a buck and couldn't budge the cart off the ground.

Ford stopped hurling the stones, shocked that someone other than Otis had finally addressed him. "In Detroit." He answered.

"That's a long way from here. What were you doing out there?"

Ford recalled his earlier life before venturing into the private investigation business.

"Sammy, I used to play ball."

"Baseball?"

Ford nodded. "Yep. Played third base for the Detroit Wolves in '32. We were pretty good, but the funds ran out."

"How come you didn't move on to another city?"

"Just didn't work out." Ford decided to change the subject. "What about you? You seem pretty young to be on this unit."

Sammy frowned. "I'm seventeen."

Ford crossed his arms and gave the youth a questioning look.

"Okay, okay. I'm fifteen but don't tell old man Crabtree. I really need the dough. My daddy was working here. He'd come home every week or so with some cash for momma and the girls. That was months ago."

"What happened?"

Sammy shrugged. "He stopped coming home. I asked Otis about it, and he just got real sad. Offered me Pa's job. Here I am. That's that."

That's that, thought Ford. Boy that sums up an entire generations attitude.

"Sammy, what happened to the men that came up here from the state?"

The boy shook his head.

"You don't know?" asked Ford.

"I didn't say that." The boy croaked. "They's gone. I heard Jenkins took them into the mine to see how it run and all, and something happened."

"Something?"

The boy struggled with his words. "Something went wrong. They says it was an accident. Mr. Jenkins told everyone to keep mum. An accident could shut us down, and that means no job for me."

"And no money." Ford concluded. He handed Sammy a stone. "Still an hour of daylight left. Want to toss a few?"

Sammy's eyes lit up. "You bet!"

Ford wound up and hurled a strike inside the circle. Sammy tried to repeat the move but his toss sailed wide.

"Guess I wouldn't have made the Wolves." He joked.

Ford chuckled. "Even a wolf starts off as a cub. Keep trying, kid. If you make something a routine, it becomes a habit."

"Aren't habits bad, like drinking?"

"Not all habits, Sammy."

Ford continued to toss strikes until it got too dark to see.

"Let's call it a night. I don't want Jenkins waking me up again."

"Amen to that, Rufus." Sammy echoed.

●   ●   ●

Rutherford Jones waited until it was pitch dark to make his way up the mountainside to explore the vast cavern that Jenkins' mining crew claimed bore no riches. He carried only a book of matches to light his way. He had already burned through a few when he reached the entrance.

"Hope you don't think you're going to enter the tunnel with a lit match?" whispered a shadow near the rocks.

Ford tensed, ready for battle.

"Whoa! Relax, big fella." A flashlight clicked on and off briefly, just enough for Ford to recognize Otis Crabtree.

"Otis, what are you doing up here?" Ford demanded in a harsh tone.

The old man shuffled around—a dark silhouette in the moonlight.

"Appears to me I'm stopping a fool from blowing himself up."

"What are you talking about?"

The old man grabbed Ford's arm and propelled him into the cavern. He pointed the flashlight beam at a storage box bunkered a few feet within the tunnel. "This place is filled with explosives, mostly dynamite but also some nitro. You walk in there with those matches, and they'll never be able to scrape up what's left of you."

Ford instinctively shoved the matchbook into his back pocket.

"Thanks, old timer. I would have involved you earlier but I have a feeling Jenkins isn't a man that takes kindly to trespassers."

"You mean the state auditors? The men were told they perished in an accident…"

Ford cut him off. "Yeah, Sammy filled me in on the tale Jenkins spun. Don't make it right, though."

Otis Crabtree shrugged. "Bunch of rich white boys put our livelihood in jeopardy, only natural my gang would go along with the ruse. It's a harsh world, Rufus."

"Yeah, I get that a lot. So it's okay for a fifteeen-year-old boy to help cover up a murder? What message you sending him?"

The elderly black man didn't respond. He aimed his beam down the path, focusing on a section of the cavern that was blocked off.

"None of my men were there, but way I hear it, Jenkins lured those city slickers inside that narrow section and then knocked them off. I suspect you'll find the bodies buried under that rubble."

Ford started toward the heap of rock and gravel, but a strong grip on his arm stopped him.

"What gives, old man?"

Otis maintained his grip. "You start kicking around that pile and you might trigger a collapse. The dust alone could choke the air out of your lungs."

Frustrated, Ford started back toward the entrance. "I'll have to come back with the proper equipment to dig those men out. Their families deserve that much."

A chorus of voices stopped them dead in their tracks. Someone was headed toward the cavern! From the sound of footsteps, it was a large group of men.

"Damn!" Ford uttered. "We're cooked! It must be Jenkins."

Otis Crabtree remained calm. He pointed to the huge pile of rubble where the state inspector's remains lay.

"You said we could bring the whole thing down on our heads!" Ford protested.

"Yes, that might happen. On the other hand, it's a guarantee that Bradley Jenkins ain't gonna let us leave this tunnel alive if he finds us. You do as I say and you'll live through this Rufus."

Ford rubbed a hand over his mouth. He didn't like the plan. He also knew he couldn't defeat a dozen men barehanded. Anxiously, he scurried after Otis Crabtree as the footsteps got closer.

• • •

The first man to enter the cavern held a flashlight and a sharp pick ax. He waved it around effortlessly like it was a pencil. The man was a giant. His bald head gleamed from the narrow beam of light.

"Son of a bitch!" Ford whispered from his hiding spot. "I know that brute."

Otis and Ford had bunkered down under a huge slab of rock inside the cavern. They were both on their hands and knees, sheltered in tight quarters among the debris.

The man Ford had recognized was Brass Knuckles, the bouncer from the Parrot. He sported a nasty shiner under his left eye, no doubt a gift from the sailors.

"Easy, big guy. I know you're itching for action first day on the job, but you have to be careful inside these mountains."

The voice belonged to Bradley Jenkins. He stood shoulder to shoulder with his new employee.

Knuckles relaxed, his grimace subsided as he bowed to Jenkins's authority. "Sorry, boss. I swear this darkie we were following looks like some joker that I owe a beating to."

Jenkins bellowed heartily. "Ah, they all look the same to me. Now put that ax down. You strike a flint in here and you might blow us to smithereens!"

The bald headed strongman relaxed his grip on the tool.

The rest of the scouting party flashed their beams around the interior of the tunnel. They found no sign of the intruders. Jenkins tired of the search after a few more minutes and rounded up his posse.

"Listen up men! We probably scared those boys all the way back to camp. We're just wasting energy up here."

The group of men all nodded in agreement, their bloodlust had evaporated in the foul air. They decided to head back and get some shut-eye while the night was still young. Jenkins left orders for a few men to stay behind and guard the entrance in case the men returned.

Jenkins grabbed Knuckles as they were heading down the mountain.

"That booze you brought from the Parrot? I got a real good idea how to put that to use."

Knuckles shot him a confused look. "Thought we were saving that for a special occasion?"

Jenkins tugged at his handlebar mustache. He twirled it deviously.

"Oh, this will be special. Very special."

•　•　•

Ford and Otis remained motionless for almost an hour before cramps and dehydration set in. The confinement was making Ford claustrophobic and he was unable to wait any longer. He slowly discarded the rubble he was hidden beneath.

"Are you crazy, son? Those guards are still outside the cave?" Otis protested.

"That's good. They won't fire at us for fear of hitting the explosives."

"Still, I don't like it."

Ford studied the man as well as he could in the darkness of the cave. It was clear Otis Crabtree had seen better days. What strength he might have possessed had been sapped in seclusion.

"Start whooping it up." Ford ordered.

"Well, why in the heck would I do that? Those boys will be here in a flash."

Ford flashed his brightest smile. "I'm counting on it old man."

A moment later Otis Crabtree was on his feet, the lack of circulation making him wobbly. He stumbled around the cavern, literally screaming toward the entrance. He didn't have to exaggerate. His pain was real.

The posted guards immediately turned their attention to the old timer as they raced into the tunnel entrance. Ford met the first man with a stiff arm outstretched. The man bounced off him dazed, a victim of a vicious neck blow. Ford belted him into darkness with a cruel right hand.

Confused, the other two guards waved their flashlights wildly around the surroundings. Otis Crabtree was still dancing around on the heels of his feet, taunting them. Ford was able to shove one of the attackers head first into the cave interior. The man's head hit with a sickening thud, and Ford was grateful for the dim light.

The last man panicked and drew his gun. He held it high above his head, the flashlight showing his crazed features.

"Don't come near me, you savages! I swear I'll unload my clip right at the dynamite."

Ford had no doubt the thug meant what he said. Any semblance of sanity had drained from the frightened man's face.

"Put the gun down." Ford instructed calmly.

The scared youth trembled. He cocked his revolver, ready to unleash hell.

"Don't do it!" Ford pleaded.

The man's finger started to squeeze the trigger when a dark silhouette snuck up behind him. He groaned once as Otis struck his skull with the blunt end of the flashlight. The gun clattered to the ground harshly. Both Ford and Otis held their breaths, but the bullet did not dispel.

"Damn! What if that gun went off?" Ford demanded.

Otis stiffened. "Well, what was I supposed to do? You were taking forever. I thought I was going to have a birthday waiting for you to do something!"

Ford shook his head in amusement. "Crazy old man. Let's get out of here. Hopefully, Jenkins hasn't done a head count back at camp."

• • •

Bradley Jenkins had indeed not conducted a head count down at the development tents. In fact, in a surprising move, he had come bearing gifts for his hard working men.

"Compliments of Mr. Peter Ellis, boys!" Jenkins and Knuckles began pouring liberal amounts of alcohol for all the men in camp. "A reward for all your hard work."

The group of black men immediately swarmed the table Jenkins was dispensing from, shouldering each other out of the way for seconds.

"Easy, men! Mr. Ellis assures me he has enough of this fine booze for all of us. Take your time and enjoy it."

One of the workers approached Jenkins, his courage bolstered from the alcohol. "You all right Jenkins."

Bradley Jenkins yanked at his mustache, a grin blooming across his face. "Glad to hear it fellah. I want to make sure everyone has a drink. Did I miss anybody?"

Most of the men ignored his question, greedily gulping the booze that Knuckles had supplied. A small throng did point at young Samson who was sitting in a corner, nursing on fresh water.

"Sammy, he ain't had none." Declared one of the more boisterous revelers.

Bradley Jenkins poured a healthy dose into a tin cup and headed over to the teenager. "Time to be a man son. Drink up."

Sammy shook his head to decline the offer. "No thank you, sir."

Jenkins was amused. "May I ask why not?"

The youth raised his eyes humbly. "It ain't that I'm not grateful, sir. It's just that I promised my mama I wouldn't touch the stuff. The devil's urine, she called it."

Bradley Jenkins guffawed mightily. "Is that so? You hear that boys? This young one said Mr. Ellis has offered you some of the devil's piss! Isn't that right boy? Isn't that what you said?"

Sammy started to shake. He could detect the anger in Jenkins' voice.

"No, sir. That's not what I meant. I didn't…"

Jenkins slapped him across the face, hard enough to dislodge the boy from his seat.

The other workers grew silent, fearful that their party might end. One of the men grabbed Sammy forcefully by the collar.

"Don't let him bother you, Mr. Jenkins. The boy's too stupid to understand he disrespected you." The man slapped Sammy harder than Jenkins had. He bent over to help the boy up.

"Keep your mouth shut!" He whispered into Sammy's ear.

Jenkins grinned; satisfied that order had been restored. He glanced at Knuckles. The bald headed man stood at attention awaiting a signal. Jenkins gave him a subtle nod.

Knuckles continued to open bottle after bottle of the moonshine. To each container he added a splash from a vile he kept under the table. No one noticed. They were too happy imbibing the alcohol.

Jenkins banged a couple of tin frying pans together.

"A toast to Mr. Peter Ellis!" he roared.

The men hollered back their approval, tilting back their heads and swallowing mouthfuls of the tainted booze.

One by one, the men grew sleepy, nodding off in their chairs. Some even passed out on their feet. Within moments, the floor was littered with bodies, unmoving.

Young Samson rushed from his overturned chair and kneeled before one of the stricken men.

"He ain't breathing!" He proclaimed. The boy crawled over to another man. "Nor him!"

Bradley Jenkins and Knuckles exchanged a look, neither confessing what they knew. The booze was tainted with poison. The workers had been murdered by the lethal concoction.

Sammy tugged and pulled at various bodies, desperate to locate a pulse. His efforts proved fruitless as he stood helpless, stunned by the turn of events.

"What did you do?" The boy demanded.

Jenkins shrugged feigning a look of innocence. "Mr. Ellis must have bought this stuff from a disreputable source. Imagine when the newspapers get a load of this. His public image will be ruined, and so will Basehart Mining."

Knuckles couldn't stifle his glee. He fought back giggles, despite a glare from his boss.

Sammy didn't buy it. "No, this ain't right. When Otis gets back…" the boy clamped a hand over his mouth, but it was too late.

"What's that? Speak up?" Jenkins raced over to the youth and circled his thin neck with crushing fingers. "What about that old dried up prune?"

Sammy gasped for air. "You're choking me…"

Jenkins rifled a fist into the boy's gut, knocking the air from his lungs. He turned to Knuckles, a feral look forming on his face. "Now we know who was skulking about up at the mine."

Knuckles extracted a gun from underneath his jacket. He opened it to show that it was loaded.

"I'll fill that old man full of holes." He vowed.

Jenkins was busy counting the bodies. He lashed out a hard kick at Sammy. The boy was still gasping for air from the punch he had taken.

"Where's that other fella? The big son of a bitch that just started. Rufus, I think his name was."

Sammy shook his head to say no. Secretly, he wanted to smile. If Rufus and Otis Crabtree were still out there, then the boy's hope for survival, no matter how slim, had just increased.

• • •

Rutherford Jones felt a chill run up his spine. The tents down at the development camp were eerily quiet. He found this odd. It was far too early for the men to have bed down.

"I don't like this." Otis remarked. He pointed at a car in the distance. "That's Mr. Ellis' wheels. Wonder what would drag him out here this time of night?"

Ford didn't wait for an answer. He burst through the entrance to the mess hall. Instantly, his knees wobbled. He felt like vomiting.

"What is it son?" Asked Otis, forcing his way past the burly man.

The old man's eyes bugged out at the horrific scene. Bodies lay scattered about, spilled cups still dripping the tainted alcohol.

"Lord in heaven! My men!"

Ford spotted Peter Ellis in the corner. Jimmy McGee was beside him. They were tending to the stricken form of a young, lean man.

"Sammy!" Ford yelled, racing to their side.

Young Samson lay cradled in his employer's arms. The boy's face was barely recognizable. He had been savagely beaten by Bradley Jenkins and his henchman, Knuckles.

Ellis looked up. He couldn't speak. He just continued to rock the boy in his arms.

"What about that dried up prune?"

"Rufus, thank goodness you're ok." Bottles McGee piped in. Despite the nature of their situation, he had remembered to use Ford's alias. "All these men, dead!"

Otis Crabtree was on his hands and knees, confirming his worst fear. "Bad moonshine!" He cursed.

Ford grabbed one of the bottles that still had some booze in it. He smelled it curiously. He then poured a drop on his fingertip and touched it to his tongue. He immediately spit it out.

"It's bad for sure, but I don't think it came that way."

The old man cringed, fearful of what he suspected. "It's poison. Aint it?"

Ford nodded in confirmation. "Someone murdered these men!"

For the first time since their entrance, Peter Ellis made eye contact with them. The man's face was streaked with tears. He was gasping trying to get out his words.

"What is it, Mr. Ellis?" Jimmy McGee inquired.

The mine owner clenched his hands with fury. "This is all starting to make sense now. My foreman, Bradley Jenkins called me earlier and suggested I throw a party for the men to boost morale. I told him funds were low, but he mentioned he had a new guy with a direct line to some affordable liquor."

Knuckles, Ford guessed.

Ellis continued, "I agreed to fund the shindig. After all, these boys work hard, and if we were going to shut down, I felt I owed them one last hurrah."

"One last hurrah," Otis cursed.

Clearing his throat, Peter Ellis continued his explanation. "No sooner do I get off the phone with Jenkins, when I get a call from my lawyer, Marion Preston."

"How does he figure in this?" Ford asked.

"He told me that a terrible accident had just taken place at the mine. Said all the men had died from a bad batch of moonshine. He said this was the final nail in the coffin. Once the press finds out about it, the mine would be worthless. Preston said it would be in my best interest to accept the offer from my rivals."

Jimmy McGee interrupted. "I thought something smelled about it, but I didn't know what to do so I told Mr. Ellis it was his call."

"It's not your fault, Mr. Jones." Ellis said to McGee. "I panicked under pressure. I have no one to blame but myself."

Ford forced himself to intervene. "What exactly did you do, Mr. Ellis?"

The young man covered his eyes in agony. He opened them again to stare at the young black boy who lay helpless on the tent floor.

"Jenkins drove the paperwork to my office a short while ago. I signed the sales contract and called Mr. Jones to take a ride up here. That's when I found all these men laying here dead."

Jimmy McGee gazed helplessly at Rutherford Jones. It was obvious the skinny youth felt responsible for the incident. Ford placed a hand on his shoulder, consoling the man.

"First off, we have to inform the police what happened here."

Ellis nodded, his runny nose making him seem younger than his years. "Already done. We stopped at a diner on the way and called it in. They should be arriving shortly."

"Good," said Ford. He turned to the old man. "Otis, I hate putting the weight of the world on your shoulders, but can you handle this?"

The old man straightened his back, forcing a grim look of determination. "I'll stay here and wait for the police."

Ford nodded and then turned to Bottles McGee. "Mr. Jones, do you know where this guy Preston has his office? It's too late to file that claim tonight. Maybe we can intercept him before the night is over."

Jimmy looked confused. It was obvious things were happening too fast for him. Fortunately, Peter Ellis interjected.

"He keeps an office in downtown Los Angeles."

Again, Ford was thinking two steps ahead. "That's quite a drive from here. We still have a chance to halt this takeover."

Ellis wiped his nose again. "Thank you, Rufus. Mr. Jones never told me you were so resourceful."

Ford ignored the compliment. "Mr. Jones is a wonderful employer, sir." He winked at Jimmy, careful to make sure Ellis didn't see him."

"What now?" Bottles McGee wanted to know.

"You and I head to Los Angeles. We can stop and call our old friend Billy O'Leary of the LAPD to see if he can lend a hand." He turned and assisted Peter Ellis to his feet. "Sir, it's best if you stay here when the police arrive. Your word will backup Mr. Crabtree's story."

"Yes, of course." Ellis replied with a whimper.

"Oh and Mr. Ellis, we found those state investigators, or at least what's left of them. Otis can lead the police to their bodies."

Ellis shook the old black man's hands vigorously. "Grandfather said you were a loyal company man."

This time, it was Bottles McGee who opined a thought.

"You know, there's something to be said for experience, Mr. Ellis. If you do get your mine back, maybe it's time you hire the right foreman to oversee operations."

Ford grinned with amazement. "Sounds like good advice."

• • •

Detective William O'Leary of the Los Angeles Police Department wasn't well liked by his superiors. That was because the rough Irishman was something of a rare bird in depression-era Los Angeles. Billy O'Leary was an honest cop among corrupt politicians, murderous gangsters and opportunistic law enforcers.

He thrived on his unpopularity.

"Yes, indeed, laddie, I know Marion Preston. A typical L.A. shyster if you ask this man's opinion. Only lawyer I ever trusted was a youth out of Harvard that works for some explorer in New York. Other than that, you can shipwreck the rest of them."

Ford and Jimmy filled him in on the details of their case. They had stopped for gas and were feeding the payphone across the street a steady diet of nickels.

O'Leary was more concerned when the topic of Bradley Jenkins arose.

"That's one tough customer, boys. You might end up in a ditch if you quarrel with him. Take my advice and let the courts settle this."

Jimmy McGee snorted. "You know Peter Ellis wouldn't stand a chance of getting his mine back."

"Sad but true, gentlemen. But at least he'd still be guaranteed to wake up in the morning," the friendly Irishman paused. "Whatever you boys decide to do, I can't get involved. The only thing I can do is make a few calls over to Redding and vouch for your report on Basehart Mine. Other than that, I can only pray the Lord delivers you safely."

Ford and Jimmy thanked him and hauled butt back to the car. They were intent on stopping Marion Preston's scheme. A dozen or more souls deserved it, including a fifteen-year-old boy.

• • •

Marion Preston was a seedy little man. Even his expensive clothing and well-groomed hair couldn't hide his despicable nature. He sat across the table from Bradley Jenkins and his goon Knuckles inside a small café outside the Hollywood Roosevelt hotel.

The waitress brought over their coffee and pastry and departed as quickly as possible. She had once lingered too long at Mr. Preston's booth and the owner had cut her wages drastically for a two week period. The young widow would never make that mistake again.

Jenkins handed over the manila envelope containing the sales agreement that he had conned Peter Ellis into signing.

"All that planning paid off," the dishonest foreman proclaimed.

Marion Preston shot him a dirty look. "At great risk, I might add." He pointed a finger in Jenkins' face. "No one told you to kill the state inspectors."

Jenkins put on his most angelic face. "Surely, you're mistaken. Those gents wandered into an excavation site unescorted. A tragic accident befell them." His look of innocence evaporated, replaced by a menacing snarl. "Ain't that right counselor?"

Preston measured his words carefully. "You did everything that was asked of you Jenkins." The lawyer faked a smile and extended his hand across the table. "It's all about results."

Satisfied, Jenkins eased up his manner. Preston was a little irritated by his foreman. He studied Knuckles with a wondering glance. Perhaps a replacement may be in order.

"The police up in Redding will have no interest in investigating the moonshine deaths of a bunch of overpaid black men. We'll let Peter Ellis suffer from some negative press and then I'll spin it that the new mining company came in and upgraded the place and struck a new silver vein. It's money in the bank boys."

Jenkins and Knuckles grinned appreciatively. The waitress returned with heaping plates of apple pie and scoops of ice cream. She smiled and scampered away before Preston could chide her.

"Enjoy your pie, boys. Tomorrow morning I'll be at city hall first thing in the morning to file the paperwork. Basehart Mining will cease to exist!"

• • •

Jimmy McGee felt his teeth chatter. It was too warm to have the shivers. He was suffering from either withdrawal or fear. He suspected it was a little bit of both.

"You don't have to do this Bottles," Ford explained. "You never signed up for the rough stuff."

Bottles fidgeted with his hands. They were parked two streets over from Marion Preston's ritzy office. The streets were filled with happy faces spilling out of nightclubs, theaters and high-end restaurants. All the men wore suits. The women were dressed to the nines.

"So this is how the high-brow crowd lives." The skinny youth marveled at the neon lights and glitz and glamour of the big city, a contrast to the shadowy docks he frequented in downtown Oakland.

"Maybe we were wrong, Jimmy. Maybe Preston will take the papers back to his house."

Jimmy McGee shook his head. "No, lawyers are a predictable lot. They thrive on order and discipline. Good or bad, Preston's got a routine. Any shyster worth his salt will pour over those documents before presenting them in front of the zoning board."

Ford was impressed by his partner's reasoning skills. "You're good, Jimmy. I'm lucky to have you on my side. You know, with a few peeks at some of those law manuals, you might make a good lawyer."

"Me? Don't be foolish. I can't even be myself. Half the time I'm you. I find myself having to remember my last name is McGee, not Jones."

"Doors are open to you that I may never enter, my friend. You should take advantage of your opportunity."

Jimmy was about to argue when they spotted the lights snap on in Marion Preston's second floor office. A small, weasel faced man approached the window and drew the shades. Probably, Preston, Ford thought.

He could make out two other silhouettes entering the office. Big ones. Jenkins and Knuckles.

Ford reached over and popped open the glove compartment. He withdrew his revolver and checked for bullets. The cylinders were full. In all the years he had owned it, the gun had never been fired.

He couldn't be sure it even worked.

"Please don't tell me things are gonna get ugly," Bottles McGee pleaded.

Ford spun around and stared at the frail man in the backseat. McGee's hands still trembled. His face was paler than usual.

"Jimmy, I need you to stay outside."

McGee protested loudly. "No way, I ain't useless! Let me help."

"I didn't say you wouldn't be. I just need to make sure your skills are put to use. First off, find Preston's car. The plate numbers O'Leary gave us will make that a snap. I need you to flatten the tires while I'm retrieving the contract."

Bottles considered his task. "I can do that, but that leaves you facing three against one odds."

"I wasn't through yet, Jimmy. I need you to start a distraction. If you can draw one of those goons down to the street, I'm sure I can handle the other. Preston, himself, should fold like a newspaper."

Bottles McGee nodded. The case of the shakes had subsided a bit. He extracted his lanky form from the vehicle and sauntered down the sidewalk studying car plates.

Ford concealed his gun underneath his windbreaker and crept along the shadows to the back of the brightly lit building. He originally had planned to wait for the group to leave, but Jimmy's speech about lawyers following a pattern had convinced him that Marion Preston most assuredly owned a safe. If those documents became enshrined in it, Basehart Mining would be dissolved!

•   •   •

Marion Preston leaned back in his expensive leather chair. He could see that his goons, Jenkins and Knuckles were practically drooling. It disgusted him to have to deal with such cretins.

"Relax, boys, I'll have your dough ready in a moment."

Jenkins fidgeted in his seat. Knuckles just stared blindly at the wall. Neither man cared much for the small framed lawyer. They were more impressed by men who posed a physical threat.

Preston thrived on their anticipation. "You know, I have a custom that I adhere to after winning a successful trial." He waited a moment to see if the men would speak up. They remained silent.

"I like to light up a victory cigar to celebrate my victory," Preston continued pulling open a desk drawer. He clawed three cigars from a wooden box and offered one to each man.

Jenkins lost his patience. "I don't smoke. Shouldn't you just lock them papers up and pay us the bonus you promised?"

Preston withdrew his expensive cigars. "That was my plan."

He made a slight gesture at Knuckles. The bald man reacted as if he hadn't seen it. Jenkins, however, did catch a glimpse. He leaped to his feet.

"What gives?" Demanded the burly foreman.

He turned just in time to see Knuckles launch a fist at his face. Instinctively, Jenkins jerked his head to the side, but he was too late and the blow slammed into his chin. He flew across Preston's desk and landed in the tiny lawyer's lap.

Marion Preston reacted immediately by grabbing a heavy paperweight of the statue of liberty and crashed it down on his foremen's head. The powerful blow rendered Bradley Jenkins unconscious.

"Washed up thug!" Preston cursed. 'Couldn't cut it with the police and sure as all hell didn't fare better as a foreman."

Knuckles checked to make sure the man was out of it.

"What should we do with his body?" The former bouncer inquired.

Preston didn't miss a beat. "We'll frame him for the Basehart murders. I'll say he was a racist and poisoned the alcohol that Peter Ellis had purchased. The police will show no love for one of their own who fell from grace. That will smooth things over with the public, and I should be able to gather up financial backers as soon as the uproar dies down."

Knuckles nodded as if he understood. "You sure are clever Mr. Preston. That fancy law school mumbo jumbo never impressed me much before, but I see things in a new light."

Marion Preston forced a wide smile. "Good, my friend. No more seedy night clubs for you. You'll be the new foremen when I re-open the Basehart Mine."

The office door burst open and Rutherford Jones came crashing through, gun in hand.

"Can't say I have any sympathy for Jenkins, but that was down and dirty," He yelled at Preston.

Knuckles moved forward, but Ford halted him with a wave of the gun.

"Back off egghead! I'll have no problem filling your ugly mug with a full clip."

Preston puffed on his cigar nonchalantly. If he was scared, he hid it well.

"Hand over that contract you smug little bastard!" Ford demanded.

Preston remained calm. "You have broken into the office of an upscale lawyer, are threatening to rob me of a legally obtained document, and pointed a weapon at us. This isn't Oakland, young man. You're in Los Angeles now. When the police arrive to find a black man holding me at gunpoint..."

Ford heard footsteps pounding toward the doorway. He glanced over to see Bottles McGee racing up the stairwell two at a time.

"I found the car, Ford!" The thin man shouted with reckless energy. "I slashed the tires on that sweet set of wheels."

Jimmy McGee lost his enthusiasm when he entered the office. Instantly, he saw the blood soaked skull of Bradley Jenkins. This caused him to lose his footing, and he tripped into Ford.

That distraction was all Marion Preston needed to swat the gun out of

Ford's hands. It clattered to the ground and fell under the shady lawyer's desk.

"Sorry, Ford!" Jimmy gulped.

Ford didn't hesitate. He saw that Preston was scrambling on his knees searching for the weapon. The burly man lunged forward to tackle the lawyer before he could recover the gun.

Unfortunately, Ford had forgotten the giant bouncer was still in the room. Knuckles closed the fingers of hands together and slammed his fists into Ford's back, knocking the air out him and sending him flat on his belly. He saw Preston grab the gun.

"Oh no you don't!"

It was skinny Jimmy McGee speaking. The frail youth had spun around the desk just in time to step on Preston's outstretched hand. The lawyer howled in pain.

Ford reached for the gun again only to have Knuckles stomp on his back. He turned over and nearly caught a foot in his mouth.

Knuckles glared at him. "I know you! You're that rube who cost me my job at the Parrot! I'm gonna kick the dark right off your body!"

With that promise, Knuckles unleashed an assault on Ford's prone body. The big man was unable to avoid the blows in the close confinement. He knew if he didn't maneuver away from the desk his life might be forfeited.

"Ford!" Jimmy McGee shouted. He had subdued the tiny lawyer as best he could.

"Get off me you flea bitten ragamuffin!" Preston cursed. "And why are you calling that man, Ford? I thought that was your name."

Bottles McGee chuckled, proud of himself for defeating his foe. His joy was diminished when he saw Ford's battered body being crushed by blow after blow. Jimmy did the only thing he could do. He released his grip on Marion Preston and launched himself at Knuckles.

Jimmy proved to be only a minor distraction, catching an elbow in the jaw for his troubles. He saw stars before finally falling. However, he had bought Ford precious seconds in which the man was able to flip over on all fours.

Ford wrapped his powerful arms around Knuckles' ankles and heaved with one last bit of desperate strength. His surge of energy caused the bald-headed bouncer to topple forward, striking his temple on the lawyer's desk. The big man twitched for a moment and then lay motionless.

"Turn around slowly." Marion Preston demanded. He had recovered Ford's gun and had it pointed at his back. "I prefer not to shot you from behind. The police might be suspicious of that."

Ford ignored him and instead his eyes sought Jimmy. Bottles McGee lay prone, his breathing was labored and a trickle of blood dripped from his chin.

"Jimmy!" Ford yelped.

'Save the theatrics." Preston ordered. "Way I see it, you're in a predicament. You can chase me and hope that I don't shoot you or you can stay behind and tend to your little friend… He don't look so well."

Ford gritted his teeth. He wouldn't abandon Jimmy. Not now, not never.

Marion Preston beamed with satisfaction. "Once I file these papers, all of this will be for naught. The Basehart Mine will be my property."

He backed away from Ford and Jimmy, never taking his eyes off them.

"Thing is I don't like loose ends. I'm thinking I'll just shoot all three of you and say Knuckles died trying to save me. That will tie up the last loose end."

He aimed the gun at Ford. There was nothing the big man could do.

The sound of the bullet was deafening. Ford's airs rung from the shock. He glanced at himself, waiting for the blood to flow, but it didn't. Instead, Marion Preston started to spew crimson from a round circular hole in his temple.

Confused, Ford looked up at the doorway.

In the frame of the door stood a masked woman with a smoking silver-plated.22 automatic. The leggy blonde wore a satin gown that clung to her hips and breasts alluringly. Ford locked eyes were her, mesmerized by the beauty of this savior.

"You!" he whispered.

"You're welcome." The sultry siren returned.

Ford couldn't believe his eyes. He had heard tales of Los Angeles' fair skinned avenger. He had thought they were a myth. He was wrong.

"Billy O'Leary is a friend of mine." The beautiful crime fighter explained. "I had a hunch you might need an assist."

Ford rose to his feet. "Thank you." He extended his hand. "I'm Rufus."

The mysterious blonde woman arched her eyebrows beneath her domino mask.

"No need to carry on your charade around me Mr. Jones. Your mother wouldn't appreciate you discarding the name she gave you."

Ford smiled bashfully. He bent over and grabbed the manila folder containing the signed contract. He looked hopefully at the stunning blonde.

"I'm not a police officer, Mr. Jones. I trust you will do the right thing." She studied the crime scene. "I usually leave my calling card at the scene, but not this time. I'm not going to steal the limelight from you boys."

There was a moaning sound coming from beneath the desk. Bottles McGee popped his head out, shaking the cobwebs from his brain.

He pointed at the beautiful woman.

"I'm dead! Must be. Only an angel could be as beautiful as you!"

Ford laughed. His jaw ached from the effort, but he didn't mind. "Don't you recognize the domino mask, Jimmy? You're looking at the Domino Lady!"

"No, I'm not." Jimmy replied.

"Of course you are." Ford began, turning to face his ally in crime, but she had vanished!

Bottles McGee dragged himself to his feet. "I guess I'm not dead, but man that was close." He looked down at the two dead men in the office. "Looks like we got some explaining to do."

Ford draped an arm around his skinny friend. "Yes, we do Mr. Rutherford Jones. We surely do."

THE END

the STOLEN SCRIPT

Jimmy McGee slammed down his coffee mug.

"I'm tired of pretending to be you."

He was speaking to his friend and boss, Rutherford Jones.

"I don't like it either," replied the muscular man. "But we both know it's necessary to keep this business afloat."

McGee forced himself to take another gulp of the scalding coffee. "Really, Ford, what's wrong with a world in which an educated black man has to pose as an employee for his drunken Irish friend?"

Rutherford Jones retrieved his friend's cup and refilled it. "Listen, kid, you know we wouldn't get any clients if folks opened that door and saw me sitting behind that desk. I don't like it, but that's just the way it is."

Jimmy "Bottles" McGee shrugged and sipped at the steaming cup of java. "This stuff is starting to give me the jitters."

"Too bad. Drink it up. The man said he'd be here any minute."

The pair were expecting a prospective client to arrive at their office. The office was an upstairs apartment in a downtown building. It also served as the men's abode. At night, they opened cots inside the small office. There were a lot of people living in far worse conditions.

It was 1936 and Oakland, California was developing in the glitzy shadow of its big brothers, San Francisco, and Los Angeles. The depression had hit America hard, and the west coast had become a haven for desperate men trying to survive. Unfortunately, that culture had led to an explosion in crime and violence. It was becoming a world of dog eat dog, and many people were forced to seek assistance outside the law.

That is where Rutherford Jones and Bottles McGee came in. The two men ran a small, but profitable, private investigations firm. No case was too small, nor too dangerous for them. They had been set up in downtown Oakland for over a year.

There was one catch to the situation, and it was a whopper. Rutherford Jones was a black man. That was a fact, something he could not, nor want, to change. However, people were skeptical to part with their money when confronted by his heritage.

To combat the problem, Ford had come up with a clever plan to fool his clients. He pretended to be a maintenance man for his friend Jimmy McGee, who in turn had decided to accept the role of private investigator.

The two men had met a few years back when Ford was shunned away from a whites-only barroom. Jimmy McGee had similarly been tossed out of the establishment for drunken buffoonery. The two men had bonded over some cheap hooch and had remained friends.

Unfortunately, Jimmy's other best friend was alcohol. He craved it with a selfish disposition. This had put a dent in the pair's business. It was tough to be in on a charade when your thoughts are clouded.

"You need to sober up!" Ford demanded. He pointed at the cup of Joe. "You'll get no sympathy from me. I have to live with the fact that you use my good name."

"What's wrong with my name?" Jimmy demanded.

Ford chuckled. "Ain't nothing wrong with your name, except no one bothers to use it. Everyone calls you Bottles."

"It's catchy."

"It's pathetic, if you ask me."

Jimmy McGee swallowed the contents of his mug. "It was your idea to let me use your name." The skinny youth wiped at his chin. "You should have let me call you Jimmy, instead of Rufus."

Ford shook his head. "If I can't use my own damn name, the least I can do is pick one I'm proud of. Grandpa Rufus was a great man. Fought for liberty. Why, he…"

Jimmy waved him off. "Yeah, yeah, I know. Your grandfather was saved by Rutherford Hayes at the battle of Fox's Gap."

Ford was about to go on one of his spiels about President Hayes' contributions to mankind when the door of their office opened.

"Hello? Is anyone here?"

The voice came from a tall, broad-shouldered young man who looked like he could handle himself. Jimmy had spoken to him briefly over the phone but hadn't gathered too much information other than the fact that youth had been referred to them.

"We've been expecting you." Jimmy McGee announced in his most professional manner. He attempted a firm handshake, but his fingers were still trembling from withdrawal. "Can I fix you a drink?"

The handsome youth shook his head. "I don't drink, sir. Frankly, in the situation I'm in, that would be the last thing I'd want to do."

Bottles McGee nodded but he wasn't paying attention. Much to Ford's dismay, his partner yanked open a desk drawer and pulled out a bottle of expensive scotch.

"I hope you don't mind if I help myself to a little pick me up?" He muttered. "Tough night, fought off a bunch of hoodlums."

The young man pulled up a chair. He looked over at Ford, who had remained in the room. "I'm anxious to explain my dilemma."

Jimmy poured himself a liberal amount of booze into his coffee mug and nodded casually toward Ford. "Don't worry about Rufus. He's hired muscle."

The nervous youth nodded. "Okay, then. My name is Leonard Slye."

Bottles stared at the man for a moment. "Can't say your name is familiar, but your face is. How did you come by our attention?"

The youth cleared his throat. "A friend of mine, Rex Ingram, vouched for you, Mr. Jones. He said to avoid the hotshot lawyers in Hollywood and go with you. He said you solved problems, quickly and without publicity."

Jimmy dared a glance over at Ford, who remained motionless with his arms folded.

"We can be trusted for confidentiality." Jimmy stated. "You mentioned Hollywood. You wouldn't be talking about Rex Ingram, the actor?"

Ford's ears perked up at the familiar name. He had assisted the well-known celebrity on a personal matter a few months back.

Leonard Slye nodded slowly. "He's a friend of mine."

Bottles McGee couldn't contain his excitement. "Hot damn! You know De Lawd himself?"

"That character made him famous all over." Leonard Slye answered, referring to the role his friend had played in the movie Green Pastures. "I had hoped to have similar success until my problem arose."

Jimmy sipped at the scotch greedily. He knew Ford would be angry, but he didn't care. The liquid caressed his throat as it traveled down his body.

Suddenly, Jimmy McGee bolted from his chair, startling both his client as well as Ford.

"I knew I recognized you! I seen you in the pictures!"

Jimmy couldn't contain his excitement. Besides booze, he spent his income on movies, taking in features every week.

Leonard Slye didn't seem startled at the deduction.

"Actually, that's why I'm here…"

Bottles McGee didn't let him finish. "I knew I seen you just two weeks ago. You was in that movie The Mysterious Avenger!" He poured himself a generous refill of Ford's scotch. "I was hoping that movie would have been about that beautiful blonde haired angel that's been running around Hollywood giving bad guys the smack down."

"You're talking about the Domino Lady. Afraid my film was more down to earth."

Jimmy blunted all thoughts of his obsession with the golden avenger from his mind and got back to business. "So you're an actor."

Slye nodded. "Actually, a crooner, but I was starting to make the move toward more film work when this disaster hit."

Jimmy gulped at his drink before a stern look from Rutherford Jones stopped him. Momentarily frightened, he returned the bottle to the desk drawer and closed it forcefully.

"Go ahead, Mr. Slye. I'm all ears."

Leonard Slye struggled for words. "The studio honchos think I have the chops for bigger roles so they trusted me with an advance copy of a script for a feature they want me to star in."

"Well, that's great news."

"Yes, it was. I couldn't wait to get home and read the script so I skipped out on a practice session and headed home to read it." The handsome youth stared right through skinny Jimmy McGee. "I made one stop. One lousy stop."

Ford wanted to break into the conversation badly, but he knew his role as Rufus prevented it. He watched as Jimmy sat back smugly, enjoying his role now that the alcohol was starting to kick in.

Leonard Slye continued. "I left Republic right before noon. We had been shooting a project since sunrise and I was light headed from hunger so I stopped in a deli to grab a couple of sandwiches to bring back with me. When I came out of the store, I saw my window was busted open and the envelope containing the script was gone. With it went my chance for a solo career."

"Damn that's harsh." Jimmy agreed. "Can't the studio give you another copy?"

"I'd be the laughing stock of the film world, Mr. Jones. I had dreams of being king of the movie world, or at least king of the cowboy films. That will never happen now if I don't get that script back."

Bottles McGee agreed with Leonard Slye's assessment. "You did right listening to Rex Ingram. We can help you and more importantly, we can do it without leaking word to the press."

Leonard Slye straightened up in his chair. "That's wonderful, Mr. Jones."

He shook hands vigorously. This time Jimmy was prepared and made an effort to give back. He could feel the young cowboy's formidable grasp beginning to crush his spiny fingers and let up.

"We'll just smooth out the details and then we can get started." Jimmy squeezed out, glad to be released from the grip.

Slye turned and nodded at Ford. "Thank you too."

Ford smiled at the young man's politeness. He had a feeling this affable fellow would make an impact on the movie world.

• • •

The script for the Republic Pictures film was entitled "The Washington Cowboy." It had been written with another actor in mind, but the studio honchos had taken a liking to young Leonard Slye and had decided to bankroll him in the lead role. The scripts were distributed sparsely and filming was to begin in a matter of weeks.

Ford and Bottles had a short deadline to uncover the mystery.

Unquestionably, their first hurdle would be to escape their office. On the first floor resided tenant Linda Mae, a second-hand jewelry broker. She ran a lucrative business fleecing Los Angeles wannabes who felt they might get a better bargain in downtrodden Oakland.

Linda Mae was a pleasant enough neighbor who, like the boys, resided in her store front. She had developed a deep friendship with Jimmy McGee based on the premise that alcohol costs less if split by two drinkers. Ford wasn't thrilled that Linda Mae supplemented Jimmy's bad habit, but she was harmless enough not to interfere in their business. Early on, both men had agreed not to let her in on their deception.

The air-headed blonde knew Jimmy's real name wasn't Rutherford Jones. He had explained that McGee was too common among the Irish and he felt it might deter potential clients. Both men had agreed that Linda Mae would address Ford as Rufus.

This had all worked well until recently, when Ford's off again on again girlfriend, Myra Ellington had returned to Oakland. Her homecoming wasn't exactly by choice. Ford had got caught up in a brawl at Myra's place of employment and they had fired her. Swallowing back her pride, she had taken up the men's offer to move in with their friendly neighbor, Linda Mae.

The office door slammed open only a few minutes after Leonard Slye had departed.

"With it went my chance for a solo career."

"Ford, you better do something about that floozy!" The cocoa skinned woman shouted belligerently.

Myra Ellington stood in the doorway of Rutherford Jones Investigations dressed only in a sheer negligee which left little to the imagination. In her hands, she held a white evening gown spotted with gigantic stains. "Look what that drunken fool did!"

Ford briefly glanced at the gown, but his eyes were drawn hypnotically to his lover's supple body. The flimsy material barely covered her ample bosom and it flowed open at the waist, giving him a peek of smooth bare skin. Underneath she wore lacey underpants.

"Stars up in heaven!" Bottles McGee blurted out, his eyes transfixed on the lovely vixen.

Myra Ellington was a natural entertainer. Her velvet voice had enthralled audiences up and down the West coast. Along with her magnificent beauty, she had been destined for stardom, until Ford had derailed it... several times.

"Calm down baby!" Ford pleaded.

"I'll calm down all right. Just as soon as you let that peroxide jewel thief know I'm not her maid. She ruined my dress on purpose."

Linda Mae barreled through the doorway at that moment. Hands on her hips, she stared defiantly at her new roommate. "There you are. I should have guessed you'd be up here teasing the gentlemen with your assets."

Ford remained stoic. Bottles smirked appreciatively.

"This girl is so ungrateful." Linda Mae ranted. "All I ask her to do is run a few errands, maybe clean up a display case every once in a great while, and she complains about a tiny mistake I made."

Veins popped out on Myra's neck. "Mistake! You booze ridden excuse for a merchant! You were so drunk you filled up the wash load with peroxide instead of soap. You ruined my expensive gown! This has to cease before she burns the place down."

"My place." Linda Mae asserted. "Which you are a guest of."

Myra's rage continued to grow. "I pay rent to you!"

Linda Mae pointed a finger in the songstress' face. "No, you work off your rent. I allowed you to move in because I felt bad for you. Don't make me regret it."

Myra tightened a fist.

Ford took this as his cue to intervene before a brawl broke out. "Myra, she made a mistake," he stated in a soft, yet purposeful voice.

Jimmy McGee forced his way into the conversation. "I'll replace that dress for you, Myra." He turned before Linda Mae could protest his generosity. "Linda Mae understands your situation." His soothing tone caused the jeweler to blush.

"Thank you, Jimmy." She whispered, planting a kiss on his bony cheek. Linda Mae snarled at Rutherford. "I blame men like you, Rufus."

Ford was taken aback. "Me, what did I do?" he stuttered.

Linda Mae shot him a look of disapproval. "Most of your kind treat their women like cattle. It's no wonder the poor dear clings to that dress like it's a passport to a better life. "

Ford had no comeback. He had learned long ago not to engage Linda Mae in an argument. The feisty blonde reveled in verbal sparring.

"Yes, ma'am."

Appeased, Linda Mae turned to Bottles McGee. "I must have mixed the bottles by mistake."

Jimmy grimaced. "Hope that doesn't mean the laundry detergent got mixed up with my stash."

Ford stifled a chuckle. He begged to tell Jimmy detergent might be less toxic than the rotgut he had been consuming.

Myra had calmed down from her emotional outburst. "I guess I'll have to audition for the cabaret dressed like this."

Linda Mae pouted. "You most certainly will not! I will not have you flaunting your God-given assets in front of the neighborhood children."

Ford closed his eyes. He forecast what was coming next. Moments later, Jimmy McGee bought into the scenario. The skinny youth was reluctantly fishing through his billfold. He withdrew a small wad of cash and palmed it to Linda Mae. The blonde's face lit up.

"I do not want this woman tempting the virtues of our young. Take her out and buy her a new gown for her audition." He pulled Linda Mae close to him. "There's some extra dough there for yourself. Maybe you might want to purchase an outfit like she's got on."

Linda Mae blushed. "James McGee! Why, that man is corrupting you as well!"

She took his money and stormed downstairs. Secretly, she was ecstatic that Bottles McGee had made the suggestion. He was finally beginning to notice that she offered more to a relationship than being a drinking companion.

Myra waited until her roommate had departed before she risked giving Ford a kiss. "Thank you, Rutherford." She shimmied over toward Jimmy

McGee. "And thank you, James. You're going to tame that filly after all!"

Bottles McGee started to answer her when Myra surprised him with a big smacking kiss on the lips.

"I'll never understand women!" He sighed, watching Myra's shapely form depart wickedly down the staircase.

Ford slapped him on the back hard. "That's just it, Jimmy. I think you are finally understanding."

• • •

Rutherford Jones and Bottles McGee poured over Leonard Slye's automobile for a couple of hours before deciding it would not reveal any clues to the thief's identity. Ford had applied a fingerprint kit he had obtained from his good friend, LAPD Detective William O'Leary, but the results were questionable.

"That was a waste of time. Do you know how many people touch this man's car on the studio lot each day? Not to mention every gas jockey he's ever encountered."

Ford agreed with the assessment and decided their next move would be to visit the scene of the crime. This avenue also proved fruitless. No one in the deli heard or saw anything related to the theft.

"What now, Ford?" Asked Jimmy, his left eye beginning to twitch.

"We keep working. Time is sensitive, Jimmy."

Ford feared that Bottles McGee was nearing his breaking point. The skinny youth could hold his liquor, but his patience wore off after a few hours without it. He was basically a functioning alcoholic. In that class, he had a ton of company. The depression had caused an entire generation of youths to roll out west in search of a better life. The brutal fact was recovery was slow. Jobs were scarce. People were literally starving to death.

The situation up North wasn't much better. Ford had heard that folks were living in tents all throughout Manhattan and that Central Park had become a breeding ground for crime and corruption. He shuddered at the thought of what those poor souls must be battling through.

It was because of these dire straits that he allowed Jimmy McGee some leeway. The boy was young, still in his mid-twenties and loyal as a hound. His drinking problem was a common affliction and a strong recommendation for the return of prohibition. Unfortunately, booze and all its encompassing revenue may have saved the United States economy, but at a great cost.

The men stopped for a lunch break. Linda Mae had fixed them a couple of bologna sandwiches on slightly stale bread. They feasted on it like they were dining at a royal banquet.

"Life is good." Jimmy reflected.

Ford nodded in approval. Their first year of operations had seen its up and downs. They had battled a turf war with the Nine Blades gang out of Chinatown. That part of Oakland was developing quickly. In only a couple of decades, almost three thousand Asians had migrated to it. They were intelligent enough to avoid the organized crime outfits operating out of San Francisco and Los Angeles, but the crafty Orientals had dug in fiercely in the dock driven ports of Oakland.

The pair had formed an impasse with Wu Chiong, the local Asian crime lord. This bond of neutrality had allowed Ford and Jimmy to operate without fear of retaliation. In fact, Ford was coming to value Chiong's assistance in feeding information down the pipeline.

Many of the patrons at Chiong's restaurant were involved in the undercurrent of Oakland's seedy crime scene. Those gangsters appreciated the Asian cuisine that their blood money purchased. Unknown to most of these scurrilous characters, Chiong's waiters and chefs were also part of his fiendish empire. They had keen hearing, and it came in handy when drunken Americans spoke too much.

Wu Chiong greeted Ford with a bow. He rudely ignored Bottles McGee.

The old man was decrepit or so he wanted you to think. Ford knew better. He had witnessed the skeleton-like thug move deceptively like an apparition.

"I reached out to my men, as you requested," Chiong informed. "You were correct to assume a lot of film crew employees dine in our humble establishment. Apparently, the moving pictures only bring wealth to the actors and actresses and not the men who toil behind the cameras."

Jimmy was cranky. "Thanks for the commentary, Wu. What do you have for us?"

Chiong refused to make eye contact with the bony youth. He felt it was beneath him to address an underling.

"Curb your dog, Mr. Jones. The rest of Oakland might be fooled by this childish charade you stage for them, but I find it offensive. We Chinese are not ashamed of our heritage."

The words stung, Ford. They were brutally honest in their appraisal. He made a what-can-I-do gesture and sat back in the chair.

"You point is taken. So do you have any leads on who might have snatched Slye's copy of the movie script?"

Chiong relaxed, content in some self- glorified victory. "My men tell me this man Slye is a talented radio personality. Apparently the studios feel he could headline a minor production. That is where the Republic connection comes in."

"Meaning what?"

"Meaning they are a minuscule, but growing company. The richer studios have been ignoring the small productions that have come out of that studio so far. It's understandable. They film short movies on a tiny budget. The key fact is that these smaller productions have been embraced by the attention-starved American public. Republic had built a budding empire."

Ford squinted in confusion. "What does this have to do with my client?"

Chiong smiled as if he was privy to some great secret.

Bottles McGee couldn't contain his emotion any longer. "Damn it you old bag of bones. You owe us some favors. We've helped pull your fat out of the fire a few times!"

Finally, Chiong turned his focus to the frail youth. "McGee, isn't it? You must be swayed by your evil drinking already for clearly you can I am not fat." The old man turned his attention back to Rutherford Jones. "Why do you allow such an idiot to be the face of your business?"

Ford sighed in defeat. "Forgive, Jimmy, please. He meant no disrespect."

"Of course I did!" McGee chimed in.

Chiong chuckled so hard he began to choke. "You Americans amuse me. I will supply you with the knowledge you request, only so you will not disgrace my abode any further." He settled back in his chair, and got his breath.

"Republic pictures is now considered a threat to the major studios. If that script becomes a success, it will make Leonard Slye a bankable commodity. Word reached my ears that several performers who auditioned for that role were quite angry at Slye's selection. One man, in particular, was overwrought with anger."

Ford perked up. "Can you tell me his name please."

"Yes, of course. The fellow goes by the moniker of Wyatt Woodside."

Jimmy rubbed at his nose nervously. "I seen that name in some of the movie credits, but I can't put a face to it."

"That would entirely make sense," Chiong announced. "Wyatt Woodside is a stuntman. He's the guy you see in the long distance shots, riding horses and jumping off roofs. The close-up shots are held in esteem for the real star of the movie."

"The studio was split on deciding who to award the contract to. On one hand, you have Wyatt Woodside, valuable studio asset who would save money by doubling as the star of the film. On the other hand, you have a talented young man, Leonard Slye, who might be the one factor that propels your studio from small time player to top of the heap. It was a tough decision."

Ford was piecing it together in his head. Woodside, the stuntman, felt his opportunity had been seized out from under him by a relative unknown. Jealousy had spurred anger which in turn had caused the vile sabotage.

"Anything I should know about this stuntman."

Chiong bared his jagged teeth. "Bear in mind, this man makes his living causing himself bodily injury. I've only seen him once in this establishment. He immediately commands attention upon entering a room, much as you do yourself, my friend." Chiong continued, "The man towers above most commoners by at least a half a foot or so. His body is similar to yours, Mr. Jones, chiseled muscle stacked upon a frightening frame. The one noticeable difference will be obvious. Whereas you have maintained your fine profile, Mr. Woodside has subjected his face to many a battering and pitfalls. He sports a nasty scar on the left side of his face, and one of his ears is smashed in like cauliflower. He's is not, as they say, a matinee idol."

Bottles McGee perked up. "The goon!"

"What?" Ford questioned.

"In the movies." Jimmy explained. "I have seen Wyatt Woodside. Sometimes the budget is so low they re-use the same actors in different roles in a movie. I've seen that scary face Chiong described in a few of the Saturday afternoon films." He suddenly grew quiet.

"What is it Jimmy?"

Bottles McGee swallowed hard. "Any time I've seen him, I remember thinking. This guy is so frightening he don't need makeup for the part!"

Chiong lifted a bony finger and pointed at the doorway.

"I would tell you it was a pleasure, but I hate to throw out such trivial vernacular. You men have what you need. I consider my debt to you paid off."

Ford nodded. "Agreed."

Jimmy McGee glared stubbornly at the eighty pound Asian.

"What are you waiting for Mr. McGee?" Chiong asked. "Oh, of course, how rude of me."

The elderly man reached into his desk drawer, momentarily frightening the bold youth. In his crumpled up hand, Chiong held a fortune cookie.

"For you, Mr. McGee. It appears your associate, Mr. Jones, makes his own fortune. You, on the other hand, might need some guidance."

Bottles accepted it begrudgingly. "Thanks, Wu, hope it's not stale."

Chiong laughed and pointed at the door. "Get out!"

The two men departed down the restaurants winding staircase and into the foyer. Jimmy cracked open his fortune cookie and tossed the shell disrespectfully into the aquarium of exotic fish. He unfurled the note and read it.

"1185 Dry Dock Avenue." He read out loud. "It's an address."

Ford nodded. "That's right. It's one of the loading docks at the pier."

"Think old Wu is having fun with us?"

"Doubtful."

Jimmy shrugged. "So what do we do?"

"We stop for gasoline and then we head down to dry dock."

• • •

Oakland's notoriously seedy waterfront had been undergoing a renaissance as of late. A couple of years back, in 1934, the Longshoremen's strike had resulted in the unionization of the west coast seaports. It had been a brutal affair, lasting over eight days of bloodshed and violence that extended all the way to US Navy. The aftermath had cleared up the import business, but like a three headed snake, crime found a way to negate the loss of revenue.

Loading docks became a haven for night time activity, including prostitution, gambling and smuggling. Wu Chiong and his Nine Blades gang had carved a niche in the profitable pie, and that led him to gift Jimmy McGee with the dubious fortune cookie.

Ford and Jimmy arrived shortly after dusk. A phone call to Leonard Slye confirmed that the sea district had become an after-work haven for the majority of men who made up film crews. Everyone from extras, to cameramen made their way down to the waterfront to get in on the action.

Jimmy banged on the metal pull down door at 1185 Dry Dock.

"Hello?" the skinny youth hollered.

After what seemed like an eternity, the rusted gate began to ascend and a bright light filled their eyes. Ford could detect heavy breathing and the muffled sound of a large crowd emanating from the back of the warehouse.

"What do youse want?" demanded a rugged looking doorman.

The fellow stood a foot over Ford, who himself, was a timorous six foot tall.

"The Chinaman sent us," Bottles announced.

The doorman leered at Ford. It was obvious he was sizing him up. Ford flexed instinctively. The unusually cold weather had forced him to don a long-sleeve short. He preferred short sleeves in Oakland's temperate climate. Jimmy had earlier noted that it made his muscular frame stand out even more than usual.

"This darkie looks like he might be up to the challenge." The doorman sneered.

Ford remained stoic, letting the situation play out.

Jimmy pounced on the opportunity. "Wu Chiong wouldn't have sent us if it weren't obvious."

The doorman shrugged reluctantly. "Ok, tiny, you head in the front. The ape has to go in the back with the rest of the meat sacks."

Jimmy gritted his teeth. "We don't care for that type of…"

Ford gripped his friend's arm tightly. "I will follow him, boss."

The tense situation defused, Jimmy headed into the warehouse, overwhelmed by both disgust and a bit of fear. He had no ideas what lay ahead of him. His apprehension eased as he entered a brightly lit section of the warehouse that was thriving with jubilation.

In the middle of the throng of patrons rested a boxing ring. Apparently, they had stumbled upon an underground fight club.

"Wu! You bastard!" Jimmy mumbled under his breath.

The skinny youth snorted out a breath of hot air before locating an empty seat toward the end aisle. The crowd was filled with riffraff of all types. Jimmy gulped with fright. This would probably not end well.

A waspish little man sitting next to him nudged him in the ribs with a sharp elbow. "Haven't seen you here before. What's your story?"

Jimmy sized up the character as a non-threat.

"Same as you chum. I like to see a couple of bruisers beat the snot out of each other, and if I can make a buck off it, more merry for me."

Satisfied, the little man turned his attention back to the ring. Two monstrous men, clad in jeans and shirtless were pounding each other much to the audience's delight.

Jimmy took the moment to scan the crowd. The Chinese contingent couldn't be missed. They occupied the front row. The second row remained empty, either out of respect or fear.

Bottles sauntered over to the front, careful not to obstruct the view of any of the bettors.

"Hiya, Denny!" He addressed one of the Asians in front.

Denny was the man's Americanized nickname. Jimmy hadn't bothered to learn the Chinese version. He probably wouldn't be able to pronounce it anyway.

The slippery mobster turned around in his seat.

"The second row belongs to Wu Chiong. You are violating his honor sitting here."

Jimmy exaggerated his sorrow. "So sorry. Does this mean I won't get an extra fortune cookie next time I visit that old fart?"

The skinny youth handed over his thin white single spaced fortune he had extracted from Chiong's cookie.

Denny didn't turn around. He simply pocketed the note.

"Speak quickly white man."

Jimmy seized his moment. "I'm looking for a cowboy, actually a stuntman. Big scar-faced dude called Wyatt Woodside."

The mention of Woodside's name caused Denny to shift in his chair.

The greasy Asian mumbled something to his companions and they all had a soft chuckle.

"Fill me in on the joke. I don't speak Shang Hai." Jimmy demanded.

Denny finally turned and faced him.

"Wyatt Woodside will be appearing shortly."

"Say again?"

The Chinese gang member repeated himself. "Wyatt Woodside will appear shortly. He's scheduled for the next battle."

Jimmy's eyebrows unfurled.

"Woodside moonlights as a bare-knuckle brawler?"

"The American dream is it not?" Denny responded harshly. "A fighting chance as you pale types like to say."

Jimmy slapped Denny on the shoulder and muttered a half- hearted thank you. The bony youth was starting to place the puzzle pieces together. Wyatt Woodside supplemented his studio income with some night time work as a two-fisted war machine.

This must have come as a double slap when Leonard Slye was awarded the movie lead over him. It all made sense that Woodside had stolen the manuscript out of jealousy-fueled rage.

Jimmy's reverie was broken up by the ring announcer's call for the next combatants. The first man introduced was met by a smattering of small, yet polite cheers. It was clear he was an unknown commodity to the ring patrons.

Bottles McGee recognized his partner immediately.

"Ford!" He shouted. "What the hell are you doing in the ring?"

A couple of Chinese goons prevented Jimmy from entering the squared circle. It was only until after Denny vouched for him that the thin man was allowed to slip through the ropes.

"Damn, Jimmy, how many times do I have to tell you to call me Rufus when we're in public?"

Ford was naked from the waist up. His well-chiseled torso resembled a Greek statue. It was clear his athletic prowess from his baseball days had never left him.

"You don't understand…" Jimmy began.

Ford shrugged him off. "Get out of the ring Jimmy. They're about to announce my opponent."

Jimmy tugged on Ford's arm, trying to pull the burly giant off the canvas.

"But you don't understand. The guy you're gonna fight is…"

The ring announcer cut Jimmy off before he could complete his statement. Before he knew what was happening, a set of yellow hands yanked Jimmy McGee back harshly. He fell on the ring apron in front of Denny's neatly polished shoes.

"Stupid dog. Do you want to get crushed like that black baboon?"

Denny planted the tip of his shoe against Jimmy's chin. The angry Irishman fought back his instinct to spit on it. Instead, he got up and brushed himself off and kneeled down to watch the battle.

The announcer made short work out of his introduction.

"Cease all wagers, please. Your champion is here. I give you Wyatt Woodside!"

The burly stuntman climbed into the ring. His bare chest was littered with bruises and scars, medals earned on and off the movie sets. He turned his frightful visage to Rutherford Jones.

"Don't matter who you are. I'm angry and when I'm angry, I feel like stomping someone."

Ford didn't hesitate. Before the announcer could get out of his way, the hulk hurled himself into Wyatt Woodside, angering both of the men.

"You jungle savage!" The announcer cursed.

Wyatt Woodside did the unexpected. He physically grabbed the announcer by the shirt collar and flung him over the top rope. The audience roared their approval. Even the normally reserved Chinamen howled with delight.

"Shall we?" Ford taunted.

A gleam of barbarism lit up in Wyatt Woodside's marble-like eyes. He rushed forward like a grizzly bear, intent on capturing his prey. Ford sidestepped the raging menace easily and hammered him a shot to the kidneys.

Surprisingly, Woodside didn't slow down. Instead, he intensified his rage and charged again. This time he came in low, toward the knees. Ford wasn't expecting the tactic and got caught off guard. The two men went crashing into the ropes. The crowd screamed with joy. An epic battle was taking place.

"That's it Ford!" Jimmy hollered. "Keep him off guard. Use your fist."

Ford ignored his tiny friend's rant. He focused on the tyrant in front of him. The sleight distraction Jimmy's voice had registered caused Ford to shuffle his attention for only a fraction of a second. Unfortunately, that was enough time for Wyatt Woodside to deliver a monumental blow.

The force of the stuntman's punch knocked Ford back against the ropes. He saw dark spots before his eyes and his nose felt flattened. He sucked in a mouthful of blood as he dodged a quick follow up.

"Stand still boy and I promise it will be over quickly!"

Wyatt delivered his orders through clenched teeth. His distorted face made his mangled appearance even more frightful. It was doubtful any movie studio would ever cast such a man in a leading role.

Ford raised both arms up facing himself, fists touching. The blockade only slowed down the next punch. It still broke through to land on his jaw.

This time, the effect caused his knees to wobble and he felt himself beginning to lose footing. This allowed Wyatt Woodside to launch a vicious punt right into his chest. Ford sprawled on his back from the force of the kick, the blood filling up his lungs causing him to choke.

"We give up!" Jimmy McGee shouted at Denny and his contingent. The Chinaman calmly lit a cigarette and smiled as he blew out the rancid smoke.

Wyatt Woodside tried to stomp Ford as he lay prone on the ground. The boot landed just a hair away from Ford's temple as he rolled out of the ring to safety. Jimmy McGee caught him in a bear hug.

"Just stay down, Ford. This isn't what we came here for."

Ford didn't answer. He couldn't. His mouth was full with blood, his own blood.

Sensing the kill, Wyatt Woodside hurled his large frame over the top rope and landed next to Jimmy with a thud. The bony youth bravely stepped between the two combatants.

"The man's been beat. You won. It's over."

Woodside would have none of it. He gripped Jimmy McGee in his powerful arms and hurled him into the front row of seats.

Denny, the Chinaman, had foreseen the move and was able to avoid the crashing form. Bottles McGee lay limply on the floor, his fingers grasping at the leg of a chair.

"I changed my mind, Ford. Kick his ass." The youth whispered before passing out.

Ford wished he could grant his friend's wish. Right now he was trying to save his own life. Jimmy had bought him a chance, and he was hell-bent on making the most of it.

Rising to his feet, the muscular black man summoned energy from his inner reserve and charged at an unexpected Wyatt Woodside. The two giants crashed against the ring canvas, the air whooshing out of Woodside's lungs.

Ford wiped the blood from his eyes and launched his own brutal assault. He fired off punch after punch into the stuntman's midsection, each blow more powerful than the last. After a moment, Wyatt Woodside staggered forward, eager to grab hold of his opponent. Ford sidestepped him like before and this time struck him in the back of the neck.

The towering stuntman gurgled his own blood before collapsing on the cold cement floor. His body twitched for a few seconds before falling into a deep state of unconsciousness.

Denny and his Chinese colleagues threw down their beer at the beaten champion.

Ford turned and grabbed the Chinese henchman by the collar.

"Let him alone! He's done for." The dark skinned warrior protested.

One of the greasy thugs held a blade to Ford's throat.

"Unhand our leader. Mr. Chiong would not take kindly to losing a member of the Nine Blades."

Ford hesitated but relaxed his grip. Denny tried to save face by spitting on Woodside's body, but it did little to deter his anger.

"Get your slimy Irish friend and take this useless carcass with you. My customers will never bet money on him again, now that he has fallen at the hands of a …"

"Hands of a what? " Ford countered, cocking back his fist.

Denny measured his words carefully.

"I was going to say at the hands of an unknown opponent. Farewell, Mr. Rutherford Jones. You may have an old Chinese fellow fooled, but Wu Chiong will not always be leader of this tong. Someday, young blood will rule the clan, and you would be best suited not to incur our wrath."

Ford wiped a stream of blood from one nostril.

"Words noted. And send Wu Chiong my thanks."

He turned to aid Jimmy in reviving Wyatt Woodside. Jimmy had obtained some smelling salt from one of the warehouse workers.

Woodside opened his eyes and blinked at Rutherford Jones.

"Christ, I'm dead and gone to hell. I knew it would be populated with natives and leprechauns."

Ford ignored the barb and helped the stuntman to his feet. "Sorry for the exchange of punches. Wu Chiong has a silly way of baiting men to earn his blood money for him. I got suckered into it."

Wyatt nodded, checking himself over for broken bones.

"Me, too, I guess. The name is Wyatt Woodside." He offered a hand to Ford.

"Ford Jones." Ford pointed at the exit where most of the throng had headed for, now that the main event had concluded. "I'd like to ask you a few questions about a missing movie script if you wouldn't mind?"

Wyatt Woodside nodded in agreement. Jimmy McGee followed them like a small puppy toward the exit, every once in awhile stopping to sip from one of the beers that had been left behind by patrons.

• • •

"Like I told you before, you got the wrong guy!"

Wyatt Woodside sighed hopelessly as he drank from a jug of water that Jimmy McGee had offered. The trio of men had retired under the safety of a loading dock canopy as the rough waters had caused a squall to come in.

Ford Jones remained silent. He had been hoping for a confession from the battling stuntman, but his stubbornness seemed to be fueled by truth.

"I'll admit, I was peeved when I found out they gave that choir boy Slye the role." Woodside continued. "It weren't personal mind yah. I just don't think the film goers will buy into a namby pampy crooner being able to saddle up against the bad guys of the old west. I think my face reflects a more accurate portrayal of the true west."

Jimmy McGee nodded. "Perhaps someday America will go for that type of cowboy, but for now the people demand a clean cut babyface. Slye fits that role perfectly."

Woodside rolled his eyes. "That he does, but that script is a winner I tell you. If the film gets made people will know the name of Leonard Slye forever."

"Not really a heroic name, if you ask me." Ford opined. "Anyway, the poor man will never get his chance if the script isn't returned. No studio will forgive a newbie who loses the script."

"They're like gold." Woodside agreed. I've been in the pictures since the silent days, and I freely admit I have never had access to an entire script. The stuntmen usually don't even get a peek at one. We just show up and prepare for whatever the role demands."

Bottles McGee was growing impatient again. The stale beer he had consumed during Ford's match had worn off. He was beginning to feel squirmish.

'Well, if you didn't snatch it, then who did?"

Woodside rubbed his chin thoughtfully. "That's a good question kid. Republic is banking on that script to make them a power player in Hollywood. Rival studios would stop at nothing to halt production of it."

Ford was confused. "They really would fire Leonard over this? I mean, he's the victim here."

Woodside laughed. "Kid, you're a tough one that's for sure. You hit like a mule, but you think like one too. This is a cutthroat business. You're only as good as your last film. Leonard Slye will have one shot at stardom, and that's just the simple truth."

Bottles crossed his arms. "How long has Wu Chiong been running a fight club at this pier?"

Wyatt shrugged. "Hard to say. I heard it was operating before the union setup. It's harmless entertainment boys. Something for the sailors to do besides picking up diseases from the local members of the female persuasion."

Ford shook the big man's hand. "Thanks for the information."

Wyatt Woodside guffawed. "Don't know what you're talking about." He winked a battered eye at Ford. "We on the same page?"

"Absolutely."

Wyatt pointed a finger at tiny Jimmy McGee. "Sorry I threw you, son. No hard feelings?"

Jimmy tugged on his suspenders. "Now I have a story to tell Linda Mae. She's my girl."

"No kidding. Good for you." He waved and headed back into the darkened warehouse. "Thanks for the battle Ford. I hope you'll consider respecting my desire for a rematch?"

Ford wiped his still bloody nose. "Not a chance buster. It's not personal, but I don't want to line Chiong's pockets with any more cash."

Woodside laughed but didn't turn around. He disappeared from sight.

Jimmy McGee was beaming.

"Why are you so happy, Jimmy? We lost the only lead we had." Ford rambled.

Jimmy McGee remained grinning. "Yeah, true, but now we've got another feather in our cap with Chiong. "

"How do you figure?"

"Simple. A few hundred people just witnessed you pound Wyatt Woodside. That makes you the new champ of this sparring club. Old man Chiong will really be tugging on his socks when word gets out."

Ford nodded. "I see that devious brain of yours spinning around. You're planning an angle on this fight game."

"Yep, for sure. Just save it in the back pocket for when we need to call in another favor with Chiong."

Ford peeked out from under the canopy. "It's drying up a little, and we can still make it to Hollywood later tonight if we drive fast."

"Good call. Let's stop home and grab a bite first."

Ford raised an eyebrow. " A hungry Irishman? You just want to show off your bump to Linda Mae."

"Well what of it? Your ugly mug could use some sympathy also. Besides, we spent a big wad of dough on those dames. Let's take them into the city for a night out."

Ford liked the idea. Myra Ellington had been patient enough, she deserved a return visit to the nightlife Ford had driven her from.

"Let's kill two birds with one stone. You ring Leonard Slye, fill him in on what happened and see if he can meet us in Hollywood tonight."

• • •

Ford and Bottles arrived just in time to break-up another of the girls' famous battles. The two women stood outside the first-floor jewelry store arguing on the stoop. Jimmy McGee suggested they keep on driving, but Ford forced him to stop.

"They're not even dressed yet!" Jimmy complained.

"...if you didn't steal it, who did?"

Ford wasn't listening. His attention was focused on the wide range of emotions the two women were displaying. For all he knew, they could be debating the fate of the free world. More likely, they were battling over a shade of nail polish.

"Jimmy!" Linda Mae screamed, spotting the frail youth. "This woman will not learn her place."

Myra Ellington rolled her eyes and pointed at her roommate as if she had just caught her stealing from a baby.

"The nerve of this flossie!" Myra barked. "You wouldn't believe what she did to me."

Ford didn't bother to ask. He knew he would have to suffer through a laborious tale. Instead, he glanced at his well- worn watch.

"Shouldn't you ladies be dressed? You did purchase new dresses?"

Linda Mae spewed venom. "That's the damn problem!"

This immediately set Linda Mae off again. She began ranting an endless stream of profanity laced barbs directed at the girl. One of the neighbors made the sign of the cross and slammed her window shut despite the humidity.

Jimmy gently tugged at Linda Mae's arm, desperate to pull the showdown from public viewing. Only after insisting he hear her plea did she agree to accompany him into the apartment.

"You better come in too, Rufus!" Jimmy demanded, eager to have Ford settle the dispute.

Myra Ellington marched past all three and pointed to two rectangular boxes sitting on the sofa.

Ford dared to ask.

"Those the dresses?"

His lovely girlfriend spoke through gritted teeth. "Sure are."

"So what's the problem?" asked Jimmy McGee. "Dames are supposed to love new dresses."

Linda Mae blurted in first. "I do love it, Jimmy. That's the problem."

Jimmy shrugged and tossed his hands up. "I give up."

Ford took the bait. "How is that a problem, Linda Mae?"

The stubborn woman turned and gave Ford a glare.

"Rufus, I would not expect you to understand, but I will try to enlighten you."

She sprinted to the sofa and removed the cover from one of the pink boxes. Gently folding back the tissue paper, she removed a stunning beaded white dress. She held the fabric in front of herself, the anger momentarily dispelled.

"That's a swell dress, Linda Mae." Jimmy ventured. He was eyeing a nearby bottle.

"Yes, it is, Jimmy."

Myra Ellington folded her arms. "I agree. " She shimmied over to the sofa and retrieved her dress from its box. "That's why I picked it out."

The siren's dress was identical to the one Linda Mae held in front of her.

"Oh boy!" Ford whispered.

"I saw it first!" Myra said defensively.

"You most certainly did not!" Linda Mae countered. "I was already trying mine on in the dressing room when that hussy copied me."

Myra snarled. "You were probably sipping from a vin inside that dressing room,"

Linda Mae covered her own mouth in shock. "You vile woman! I don't know why we put up with you!"

Bottles McGee had snuck into the kitchen and poured himself two fingers. He threw it back and let out a hushed belch.

"I don't see a problem. Do you Ford?"

Ford didn't know where Jimmy was going with this, but he played along.

"Me neither." The dark skinned giant proclaimed.

Myra shook her fists in a tantrum. Not to be outdone, Linda Mae slapped at her own forehead. Simultaneously, the women chimed out.

"Men!"

Ford couldn't deal with it. He reached for Jimmy's bottle and took a deep slug. Jimmy smiled and reached out for a refill. Ford obliged.

"What we have here ladies is not a dilemma." Jimmy McGee announced. "No, sir, what I see is two beautiful ladies that share the same taste."

Ford nodded. "What he said."

Jimmy continued. "Look, it's simple. You both saw this dress and loved it. I think it's a great sign that the store had one for each of you. I say you both wear it."

Myra Ellington hazarded a glance at her roommate.

Linda Mae seemed receptive to the idea.

Jimmy pounced on the silence. "Then it's settled. Now you too women hurry up and get dressed. Ford and I are going upstairs to toss on our suits."

The women didn't protest. They simply grabbed their dresses and headed into the jewelry store showroom which doubled as their bedroom.

Ford stared at Jimmy. The skinny boy was sad.

"Now why are you pouting?" Ford asked.

Bottles McGee winced. "They never even asked about our bruises."

Ford chuckled. "Get up the stairs before they come out and give us some new ones."

• • •

Leonard Slye had agreed to meet them at the Blue Iguana, a well established restaurant in downtown Los Angeles. The handsome crooner was seated in a private booth unaccompanied.

Jimmy made short work of the introductions and suggested the ladies seek out the powder room. Linda Mae thrilled at the opportunity. It had been years since she had visited the city of bright lights, and the experience was a joy to her. Myra had already been prepared by Ford to give them some time alone to converse with their client.

Jimmy had agreed to curb his drinking. He knew the case might hinge on his ability to communicate with the young actor.

"So how come a good looking dude like you is all alone tonight?" Jimmy inquired.

Leonard Slye didn't hesitate. "I'm not in a relationship right now Mr. Jones. I'm focusing on my career goals at the moment."

"Yeah but with your looks and your singing chops, broads must be throwing themselves at you."

Slye was drinking tonic water. He sipped at it slowly.

"I hope to make it in the movie world, Mr. Jones. One of the things that entails is being looked upon by young folks as setting a good example. Now I appreciate the heavenly form of a woman just as much as any red-blooded man, but I'm not going to flaunt my success in front of the public."

Ford didn't like Jimmy's probing. He stared at the two men. It struck him suddenly that Slye and Bottles were exactly the same age, twenty-five. A somber mood set in as Ford realized what a difference in lifestyles the two men had. Jimmy had been exposed to the harsh elements of a bowery upbringing, his pale and lithe form seemingly waging a never-ending battle against malnutrition. While, Slye had the perfect complexion of a young man that hadn't endured hardship of any type.

It was no wonder Republic pictures wanted this man to be their lead. He was the poster child for hope and inspiration.

"Mr. Jones, why don't you tell the gentlemen what happened when we encountered Wyatt Woodside." Ford prompted.

Leonard Slye shocked him when he piped in.

"Yes, Mr. Jones why don't you fill me in."

He retained eye contact with Ford as he spoke the words.

"I think the jig is up," Jimmy muttered.

Slye leaned back and sipped at his tonic water again.

"Relax, boys," he said. "My buddy Rex told me all about your setup. Honestly, it saddens me that you have to use deception to get clients, but I understand."

Ford was relieved. He thanked the young cowboy and filled him in on the encounter with Wyatt Woodside. He toned down the violence somewhat and made no mention of Wu Chiong. Slye had listened carefully. He agreed with Woodside's reasoning that Republic Pictures, rather than Leonard Slye, might be the true target of the sabotage.

He agreed to let them shadow him the next day to see if they could dig up some leads. In the meantime, he insisted they accept his generosity as their hosts for the evening.

"I envy you boys," Leonard Slye stated.

Jimmy spilled his soda. He had rejected the offer for something stiffer.

"Say again? You're the guy with the golden voice and movie star looks. How could you possibly envy two mugs like us?"

Slye stared past them. His eyes had drifted to the Iguana's side-room where the two girls were returning from.

"You're a pair of lucky men to have such pretty ladies in your life."

Ford turned to take in the view. He was never shocked to see Myra Ellington command an audience. The sultry vixen had natural stage presence. She was a natural born entertainer and her coffee colored skin and voluptuous body distracted men on a daily basis. No, what bewildered Ford was how well Linda Mae had cleaned up.

Although she was a full ten years older than Jimmy, the youth's tough life and strong drinking habits had always made them appear similar in age. Yet now, standing before them, refreshed and made up by Myra, Linda Mae was a vision dressed in white.

Jimmy hadn't failed to notice.

"Saints alive!" he whispered.

Linda Mae caught his enthusiasm and blushed. She giggled and clutched Myra's hand like a school girl. Myra was stunned to find herself pleased by the gesture. She had battled endlessly with Linda Mae since moving in. Now she felt a kinship of sorts. She was happy they had worn the same gown. It gave her new friend a bit more confidence.

Leonard Slye called over the waiter and handed him a small wad of money.

"See that my friends enjoy themselves tonight."

Jimmy McGee tore his eyes away from Linda Mae.

"You're leaving already? The night is young."

Leonard Slye smiled and remembered his place. "Forgive me, Mr. Jones. I still work my radio program with my bandmates. I've got to get some shut eye."

The virile actor shook Ford's hand. "Rufus, it was a pleasure to see you again." He turned and faced the girls. "If you lovely ladies will give me my leave."

Myra Ellington nodded politely. Linda Mae couldn't help herself. She pinched young Leonard Slye's face.

"You handsome man. I hope to see you every Saturday."

Jimmy McGee's mouth opened wide.

"At the movies, of course." Linda Mae corrected herself.

Slye wished them all a good evening and then departed the way he had arrived, alone and without fanfare. Ford had a strong suspicion there wouldn't be many more nights like that for the talented youth.

• • •

The evening played out like a fairytale for Jimmy McGee and his date Linda Mae. They danced and laughed, dined on exquisite delicacies, and enjoyed each other's company…all without the aid of alcohol.

"Linda Mae, you sure look swell this evening." The gaunt youth complimented.

The blushing blonde squeezed his hand with joy. "It's like a dream, Jimmy. This place is so beautiful. And this night, I never want it to end."

Jimmy peered deep into her eyes. "Me, neither, babe."

He truly meant those words. Times had been tough and he treasured his partnership with Ford, but this was different. Linda Mae made him feel important.

"Let's get some air." He prompted.

The pair left by the side exit which led to a private alleyway where one of the busboys was puffing on a cigarette during his break. The youngster gave a polite wave to Jimmy and Linda and stepped back into the kitchen to give them some privacy.

"The Blue Iguana is a little out of your league, Jimmy. That was kind of Mr. Slye to pick up tonight's tab."

Jimmy agreed. "That's why I didn't order no booze. Wouldn't be right to saddle him with extras."

Linda Mae smiled coyly. "Is that the only reason?"

Jimmy thought about it.

"No, not really. Truth is I didn't want one." He placed his hands on her shoulders. "I was having too much fun."

He started to draw her close to him when he heard the sound of approaching footsteps. The pair turned to glimpse a pair of heavyset men blocking their exit. Jimmy recalled seeing them earlier. One of the men had glared at Ford and Myra and mumbled an obscenity under his breath.

"Look what we have here." The ringleader spouted, circling the frightened couple. "It's those friends of the spear chucker."

The man's partner balled his fist and slammed it against his palm. "That's right Eddie. These two love to mingle with the darkies."

Eddie continued to circle like a jackal sizing its prey.

"We don't want no trouble." Jimmy McGee stated his voice straining.

"Is that so?" Eddie mocked. "Then why would you choose to spend your time with those savages?"

His partner continued to slam his fist into his palm. With each smack, Linda Mae trembled.

"Please, Jimmy, let's get out of here!"

Eddie poked her hard in the chest. "You're not going anywhere toots."

Jimmy rushed forward only to receive a face plant. Big Eddie shoved his palm into the skinny youth's face, knocking him back a foot.

"Easy, toothpick boy! I'm just gonna have some fun showing your girlfriend here what a real man feels like."

Linda Mae slapped him as hard as she could.

"You shouldn't have done that sister. I don't take kindly to dames that put up a fight."

Eddie raised his hand as if to give Linda Mae a backhand. He was too slow as Jimmy propelled himself in front of her. The skinny Irish youth took the blow to his cheek.

"Jimmy!" Linda Mae shrieked, hysterically.

Jimmy McGee swung wildly, missing his larger opponent.

"Finish this sewer rat off Eddie. I want to pucker up with the loud mouth. I like a woman that's feisty."

Big Eddie delivered a crushing blow to Bottles McGee that sent him sprawling to the hard pavement. The fragile youth tried to rise up to his knees but collapsed back down. He was defeated.

Linda Mae refused to submit meekly. She kicked Eddie in the shins, hard. The thug moaned and gritted his teeth.

"That was your last warning." He balled a fist, ready to strike Linda Mae.

He never struck his intended target. Instead he felt a firm grip on his shoulder as he was spun around. He barely registered the face of the clean-cut man in front of him, before Big Eddie felt a fist crash into his jaw. He caved in like an ice cream cone, slumping down on his backside.

"You lousy..." began the riled up partner, only to suffer a similar fate. He was clipped on the jaw by an overhand right, and then just for extra measure received an uppercut to the jaw. He toppled over, falling on top of Big Eddie.

Jimmy McGee staggered to his feet, eyes blurry. "Who? What?"

"I'm sure you could have handled those goons, but I thought you might need an assist."

The even toned voice emanated from the familiar visage of Leonard Slye. He had returned to the restaurant, remembering he had left his brand new Stetson at the coat check window.

"Thanks, Mr. Slye," Jimmy muttered making sure Linda Mae was unharmed.

Linda Mae proved she was unhindered as she planted a wet smacker on Leonard Slye's lips.

"Mr. Slye, you are indeed a matinee idol." She swooned.

A crowd had gathered, stirred up by the commotion. Rutherford Jones and his date, Myra, muscled their way to the front of the throng.

"Jimmy, Linda Mae are you okay?" Ford inquired, genuine concern in his tone.

Before Jimmy could answer, Leonard Slye intervened.

"Everything is fine, Rufus. Mr. Jones and his lady friend were rudely interrupted by some hooligans but the situation has been resolved."

Myra Ellington leered at Big Eddie's sleeping form.

"That's the creep kept staring at me. Gave me the willies!" She hugged Linda Mae. "I'm glad you're not hurt, honey."

Linda Mae returned the hug. "I feel better knowing we have friends like you, Rufus and Mr. Slye." The woman straightened out Jimmy's bow tie.

"I didn't get to finish what I wanted to say." Jimmy began.

The curvy blonde raised a finger to her lips. "Shhh. You will, Jimmy. I promise." She gave him a quick peck on the cheek.

In the midst of the confusion, Leonard Slye had snuck off.

Jimmy McGee tossed Ford the car keys.

"Rufus, would you mind driving? "

Ford caught the key-ring. He wanted to say something sarcastic. He wanted to tell Jimmy that he was finally sober enough to drive, but he couldn't bring himself to spoil the moment. Instead, he grabbed Myra and set off to retrieve the car.

• • •

The early morning sun was pleasant as Ford wheeled his sedan into the parking lot of the radio station. Jimmy McGee sat in the back, his bruised face healing after a good night's sleep.

"Are you sure it's okay for me to tag along?"

The sweet melodious voice drifted from the sexy lips of Myra Ellington. The lounge singer had pleaded with Ford to accompany the pair to Slye's radio station.

"You're fine, darling," Jimmy responded. "I ran it by Leonard Slye before heading out here."

Myra perked up. "Mr. Slye is a big shot around here. His band and he are well known in the music world."

"Thank goodness for that, because if we don't locate that missing script soon, he'll be stuck on the radio for years to come."

Ford chuckled hysterically.

"What are you laughing about you big lug?" Myra asked.

"I just find it funny."

"Find what funny."

"That someone could be disappointed with the fact that they're just a radio star. I mean, that pays a boatload of green."

Jimmy McGee slapped Ford's shoulder. "True enough my good man, but Slye has that little edge. That's what gives him so much potential. Plus, he's a good, honest Joe. He deserves this opportunity."

Ford nodded. "Can't argue with that."

They exited the car and strolled to the modest station's entrance. The interior waiting room betrayed the exterior's dinginess.

"I thought we had the wrong place," Jimmy muttered.

The trio was greeted by a well-dressed gent in an expensive suit. He was a slim, pale-faced man. It was obvious he spent most of his time out of the daylight.

"You must be Rutherford Jones." The man stated, greeting Jimmy with a warm handshake. "I'm Jerry North, Leonard's agent."

"Not what I expected for a big shot radio station," Jimmy informed, neglecting to introduce his companions.

North smiled. "I hear that quite a bit, Mr. Jones. I'll let you in on a trade secret. If we advertised this place with signs out front, we'd never get any recording done. People would be banging on the door all day insisting they were the next big thing."

"Makes sense." Jimmy strained his neck. "Where's Leonard Slye?"

"The Sons and he are in the recording booth right now. Want to watch?"

"Oh, can we?" Myra piped in.

Jerry North turned and drank in her appearance. She was modestly dressed in a bright canary dress respectfully covering her full length from top to right below her knees. Even so, the girl's fabulous body couldn't be hidden beneath the agent's thoughtful notice. The top of her dress clung to her heaving bosom and her hips strained against the material.

North found himself mesmerized.

"I'm Rufus." Ford barked. "And this is my woman, Myra."

The muscular private investigator stepped in front of the songstress and gripped North's hand in a firm handshake. His eyes were serious but not threatening.

"Excuse my manners." North sputtered. "Please to make your acquaintance." He turned to Myra, a bit more formal in his approach. "You are welcome to view Mr. Slye in action."

Myra detected the man's nervousness as he strode away. She jabbed a sharp elbow into Ford's rib cage. "Must you be so rude?"

Ford made a queer face. "What?"

Myra waved a finger under his nose. "Don't start that jealousy routine again. I swear every time a fellow turns his head in my direction you're ready to bite it off."

"Nonsense."

"Maybe she's right Ford," whispered Jimmy.

"Oh, not you too."

The skinny youth raised his index finger to his head. "Let's see now. How many jobs has Myra lost because of you? There was…"

Ford reached out and shoved his partner forward. "Just follow the man before I make you end up losing your job."

They hurried down the hallway to catch up to Jerry North. He stood outside a large glass room which served as the radio station's broadcast and recording booth.

Leonard Slye was inside, crooning into a standing microphone. He was surrounded by his musical partners as well as a gentleman in a thick wool suit.

"Who is that guy with Slye?" asked Jimmy.

A frown swept across Jerry North's face. "That's the fellow that writes our check."

Ford stared at the heavy set man. "He appears to be dressed a little too warmly for Los Angeles."

Jerry North chuckled. "He dresses like that all year long. The guy is tight with a buck."

Jimmy shot him a questionable look.

"Don't get me wrong, Mr. Jones. I don't mean to turn up my nose at our benefactor, but Arthur Woolsey isn't paying the Sons a fair wage."

"What do you mean sir?" Myra chimed in.

North turned at the opportunity to address her. He didn't need to be prompted to take notice of her.

"Leonard Slye is a national draw. His music is being played all over the west coast."

"That's a good thing, isn't it?" piped in Jimmy.

North nodded. 'Sure it is, especially for Arthur Woolsey. Times are changing my friends. Sponsors are looking to back motion pictures. Arthur Woolsey has been riding a tidal wave of income for years. He's been paying his talent penny on the dollars."

"And now the picture studios are offering that talent more money."

"Damn, skippy! It was my idea for Len to try out for the movies. He's had a few roles so far, but if this film with Republic comes through, well… the sky is the limits."

Ford became suspicious. He eyed the roly-poly station manager. Woolsey was dripping sweat from his temple. He didn't appear to be in a pleasant mood.

"Why the long face?" Ford asked.

Jerry North turned and studied Ford. It was out of line for a hired hand to speak, but the agent sensed an understanding between the investigator and his beefy assistant.

"Woolsey has been in an upset mood all week." The agent stated. "Ever since Leonard started accepting film work, he's had to cut back on his recording time. As a result, Woolsey has been settling for less output from the Sons."

"And less music means less money for tubby." Myra snarled.

Jerry North turned and faced the trio aggressively.

"What gives with you folks?"

"Beg your pardon?" Jimmy countered.

"You can't kid a kidder." North protested. "Forgive my bluntness, but you two don't act like typical…"

"Typical black folks?" Myra finished.

North blushed. "Guilty."

Jimmy McGee salvaged the situation. "I provide a service, Mr. North. Men like Leonard Slye value that service. He's only interested in results."

North gulped and composed himself.

"No disrespect intended, sir." He pointed to the gentleman who was shaking a fist at Leonard Slye and his partners. "I think Woolsey is about to blow his top."

"And what would set him off?"

"I instructed Leonard to make a few demands today."

"What type of demands?"

North adjusted his tie.

"I told him to demand a respectable wage."

Myra pointed at the blubbering station manager. His face was turning red and the veins in his neck were protruding.

"I don't think he likes your terms."

Ford grabbed Jimmy McGee aside.

"Bottles, I think we have our prime suspect."

•   •   •

An hour later, Leonard Slye emerged from the recording booth. His manner and appearance were as fresh as they were at sunrise. He loved recording. Music was in his blood.

"Charmed to see you again, Myra." He drawled.

The sultry siren melted at his words. She had been around movie stars before, but none with the wholesome charm of Leonard Slye.

"Thank you." She dribbled out in amazement.

Slye shook hand with the two men before returning his attention to the curvy Myra Ellington. He was a true gentleman and never let his eyes stray down.

"My partners tell me you've been keeping a secret," he said to the beautiful cocoa-skinned woman.

Ford and Jimmy looked wonderingly.

Leonard Slye pointed at his companion musicians.

"The boys get out a bit more than I do, I'm afraid," he explained. "Seems you were a pretty big draw in Oakland these last couple of years."

Myra's eyes bulged in astonishment. "Those boys said that?"

Slye nodded. He neglected to tell her that she had been spotted singing at questionable establishments.

"Would you like to come in and record with us?"

Myra felt her knees wobble.

"But I don't know your type of music, Mr. Slye. I'm a jazz singer."

The members of Slye's band chortled out loud.

"Honey, music is music," Slye responded. "We have a particular style that the station pays us to perform, but that doesn't mean we can't enjoy all types of music."

Myra relaxed. She sought Ford's attention. He could see she was seeking approval.

"Are you sure Mr. Woolsey will be okay with this?" Ford asked.

For the first time since he had met him, Ford noticed an unpleasant look cloud Leonard Slye's usually bright demeanor.

"I'm not too fond of that man right now."

Jerry North interrupted. "He scoffed at the price?"

'Scoffed?" Slye responded. "I wouldn't exactly put it that way. He threatened us with legal action and said he'd cut our pay if we ever spoke out of line again."

The hair on the back of his neck bristled as North shook his hands.

"That tub of lard!"

Leonard Slye raised a hand in protest. "Please, Mr. North. I ask you to refrain from cursing in the presence of a lady." He turned back to Myra. "Go in and mingle with the boys. You'll be surprised at the range of music they can perform."

Myra shimmied her way past the handsome cowboy much to the delight of his bandmates.

Ford turned to Leonard Slye.

"Wyatt Woodside told us that the studios are possessive of their scripts. How many people knew you got that offer?"

Slye turned to his agent.

North cleared his throat. "Myself of course. And the Sons."

"Anyone else?"

Both Leonard Slye and Jerry North turned their heads slowly in the direction of the departed Arthur Woolsey.

"I thought I could use it as leverage in negotiating on your behalf," North explained.

"That's okay, Jerry. I'm not angry with you," Slye answered sincerely.

Jimmy McGee slapped his hands together.

"So all we gotta do is tell the studio that Woolsey is the culprit."

Ford shook his head. "I don't think Mr. Slye wants us to do that."

Leonard Slye shrugged his shoulders. "It's like I explained to you boys before. If I admit the script is lost, no matter what the circumstances, Republic will shun me like a plague."

Jerry North nodded in agreement.

"So what do we do?" Jimmy begged. "Do we just go over and demand he return it?"

Slye looked toward North for advice. The agent expressed his dislike of the idea.

"Woolsey's a bitter man. You can tell from his appearance, he's been enjoying the fruits of his success for years. I think if you confront him, he'll destroy the script out of spite."

"Maybe he already has?" Ford winced.

Jerry North shook his head adamantly. "Highly doubtful. Arthur Woolsey is a cruel unjust man, but he's not an idiot. That script is bankable, and he knows it. Sooner or later, some studio is going to steal my client. That script is Woolsey's insurance policy."

"So how do we get it?" Jimmy McGee wondered.

North rubbed his chin. "Well, besides a juicy steak and a truckload of money, he does have one weakness."

'What's that?" Ford demanded.

Leonard Slye and Jerry North locked eyes, and then both men turned toward the recording booth and simultaneously pointed at the dreamy figure of Myra Ellington.

The songstress caught their glimpse and winked back, thinking they were signaling their approval.

"Oh boy!" cursed Ford.

• • •

Myra Ellington forced her way back into the car. "I'm not doing it!"

"But you said you would!" Ford argued.

They sat in Ford's sedan, engine idling, parked across the street from Arthur Woolsey's house.

"A girl is allowed to change her mind." Myra protested.

Ford pointed a finger in her face. "No, you're going through with this. Leonard Slye went out of his way to get you this opportunity."

Myra rolled her head. "Opportunity? To be groped and slobbered over by that fat pig?"

"No, to audition for a job," Ford answered. "A job doing what you love most…singing."

"Rutherford Jones, don't you try to pull the wool over my eyes! You just want me to distract that tubby while you search his home for that damned cowboy script."

"True," Ford admitted. "But the audition is real. C'mon baby, even if this guy is a scumbag, he runs one of the most successful broadcast stations in the industry. You could be a star!"

Myra softened up. "You think so?"

"Baby, I know it. I've seen you perform. You knock 'em dead every time. And let's not beat around the bush, you've performed in front of worse creeps than Arthur Woolsey."

She sighed and checked out her reflection in the mirror.

"Let's do this before I chicken out. How do I look?"

Ford gazed lustfully at the diva. She had changed into a sequin dress with a plunging neckline that displayed her wonderful assets. The dress hugged her body before breaking off into a daring slit that showed off her amazing gams.

"You look like a million dollars!" The muscular man whispered.

Myra beamed with confidence and exited the vehicle before her courage could wane. She approached the gigantic mansion, shoving her trepidation to the back of her mind.

"Look at these digs, Ford! The man is loaded."

"Yeah, too bad he doesn't share the wealth."

Apparently, Woolsey didn't employ a butler, as the portly man opened the door himself. He was outfitted in a formal tuxedo, the crisp white shirt straining against his belly.

"Good evening Miss Ellington. I commend you on being prompt. Time is money in the music business."

Myra feigned a smile. "I want to thank you for this chance. It means so much to me."

The portly station manager waved at her impatiently. "Nonsense my dear. Those boys down at the station are talented musicians and they were enchanted by your voice. I have a hunch you'll delight me."

Ford took exception to Woolsey's tone and cleared his throat loudly. Woolsey barely acknowledged him.

"I'm afraid your chaperone will have to wait in my library. I like to evaluate the talent in private."

Ford gritted his teeth but remained silent. He wanted to stuff the windbag in a closet.

Myra sensed the animosity and intervened.

"That will be fine, Mr. Woolsey. Rufus understands the importance of this evening."

Woolsey relaxed. "Of course, my good man, you are welcome to browse the vast volumes I have amassed over the years. I'm a lover of music first and foremost, but my literary collection is very unique."

Ford nodded graciously.

"Second door on the right, young man. I excused the help tonight. I find they distract my thoughts when I'm auditioning."

"Not a problem, sir." He turned to Myra. "I'm just a shout away Miss Ellington."

"Thank you, Rufus. That will be all."

She locked arms with Arthur Woolsey and headed him away from the library. She made sure the station manager wasn't looking as she turned back and mouthed to Ford, "I love you."

•   •   •

Rutherford Jones forced himself to turn his attention to the task at hand. It turned his stomach sour to know his beautiful girlfriend was alone with that slimy con artist, but he knew Myra could handle herself. She was no slouch when it came to physicality.

The dark skinned private investigator marveled at the efficient library Woolsey had obtained. There were volumes on science and history as well as row after row of literary classics. Ford inspected the books closer. Very few of the spines were cracked. Arthur Woolsey was not a voracious reader.

He focused on the roll top desk that anchored the room. It was a large wooden one that must have traveled a path from the east coast all the way to California. It had to have been a couple of centuries old, but the frame was sturdy and pieces intact.

Ford tugged on the drawer. It was locked. He cursed under his breath and searched for something to jimmy the lock.

•   •   •

While Ford Jones was prowling through Arthur Woolsey's library, the station manager, himself was in a state of ecstasy as his eyes feasted on the sultry form of Myra Ellington.

"What would you like to hear first?" she asked innocently.

The huge man had lured her to a private study that doubled as his audition room. Its furnishings were sparse. There was only a worn sofa and a standing lamp. It was as if the room had been set up quickly. Myra could see scuff marks on the floor. Furniture had been moved around recently.

"What's your hurry darling?" Woolsey inquired. "I know your voice is heavenly. I listened to the tape before I left my studio tonight."

"You did? And what did you think?"

Woolsey patted the sofa cushion next to him. "Join me sweetheart."

Myra obeyed plopping down next to him. She could detect the faint smell of cologne, but it did nothing to mask the sweat which was pouring down his neck. She shuddered with contempt.

"I have a few melodies I could start off with." She suggested.

Arthur Woolsey draped a damp arm over her shoulders. Repulsed, the girl retracted her form as far over as possible.

"Relax, honey. I'm just trying to make you feel comfortable."

Myra remained composed. "Oh, I'm comfortable." She gently pushed his arm away.

"How about a little kiss?" Woolsey begged.

"Let's be professional, sir." She countered.

Woolsey wasn't deterred. "I can make you a star. You know, I have contacts at the movie studios."

"Is that so?"

His chest heaved boastfully. "Sure is, that's how Leonard Slye got his big break in those matinee productions. I don't really go in for that kind of stuff, too juvenile for my taste, but I understand the fascination."

Myra hoped to keep him talking. She squirmed away as his hand drifted to her knee. She prayed Ford was making some progress.

"Aren't you afraid Mr. Slye will leave your station if he becomes a movie star?"

Woolsey was taken aback.

'Young lady, you sound just like that shyster, Jerry North."

"What do you mean?" She was relieved to have deflected his physical longings for the moment.

Woolsey was only too happy to oblige her.

"*...she mouthed "I love you."*

"That two-bit agent of his has been trying to turn Leonard and the Sons against me for quite some time. You see, Myra, I value talent and those boys have got boatloads of it. I offered a very fair wage increase, but Jerry North turned it down."

Myra was intrigued. 'Why would he do that?"

Woolsey shrugged. "Who knows? I even offered to work around Slye's shooting schedule. You know he could film during the day and record at night, but North blocked that idea."

The big man reached for her again. "But who cares about those boys? I'm interested in real talent like you have." He stared at her well-rounded breasts.

"I don't think this is going to work, Mr. Woolsey."

He puckered his lips and closed his eyes.

"Nonsense, sweetheart. Now just lay one on my lips."

Myra struggled to extract herself from his embrace. The man's bear hug was powerful, and she began to get nervous.

"Please, sir, you're hurting me!"

Woolsey ignored her protests. "Just a little kiss for Arthur, what do you say?"

The door to the study swung open. Rutherford Jones breezed in, a large almanac in his hands.

"Wonderful library, Mr. Woolsey. This here book is full of pictures! And it's heavy. Very heavy."

Ford's tone was menacing. Woolsey didn't need any further prompting. He brushed himself off and rose to his feet.

"It's getting very late, and we start early in the radio business." He turned to Myra. "I will get back to you soon with a decision."

Ford handed him the volume. He held it a few seconds too long.

"You have a very nice house. It was real easy to find."

Arthur Woolsey gulped.

Myra Ellington grinned and shimmied out of the room. She put a little extra emphasis into her sway to tease Arthur Woolsey one last time.

"Good night, Mr. Woolsey."

She blew him a kiss.

The bloated station manager simply wiped the sweat from his brow, thankful his guests were leaving.

•   •   •

Leonard Slye and his agent, Jerry North, entered the quaint offices of Rutherford Jones, Private Investigator. Jimmy McGee sat behind the desk in his guise as a private dick. He had mastered the deception of pretending to be Ford's boss. Ford, himself, stood stoically in the corner, content to continue his role of Rufus, office assistant.

"Good morning, gentlemen," Jimmy called out, a natural smile gracing his face. While Ford and Myra had visited Arthur Woolsey, the skinny youth had spent a quiet evening alone with Linda Mae. Nothing could ruin his jubilant manner.

Jerry North was impatient.

"It was a long drive into Oakland this morning, Mr. Jones. I hope you have a good reason for summoning us?"

Jimmy maintained his pleasant mood.

"I have finished my investigation of Mr. Slye's case."

Leonard Slye expressed his anxiety. "Did you find it? Did you find the script?"

Jimmy turned to Ford who had crossed his arms and was glaring at Jerry North with a piercing gaze.

"It isn't quite that simple, Mr. Slye," the thin youth explained. His gaunt body still looked tired even though he had enjoyed a comfortable sleep.

"What's so difficult about it?" Jerry North demanded. "You either found the script or you didn't."

Rutherford Jones unfolded his arms and deliberately moved closer to the angry agent.

"You know we didn't find it. Just as you knew Wyatt Woodside and Arthur Woolsey didn't have it." Ford accused.

Leonard Slye scrunched up his nose. "Am I missing something fellas?"

Ford answered him while maintaining eye contact with North.

"You mean besides your movie script?" Ford answered. "Perhaps, Mr. North would like to address it with you?"

Startled, North backed away from the towering man.

Ford inched closer to the man, intimidating him with his massive frame.

Leonard Slye sensed the urgency in the room. "Will someone fill me in on what's happening?"

Jimmy McGee rose from the desk and ventured over to the door, which he slammed and locked.

"Let me give it a whirl." He began. "Leonard, you've already explained how difficult it is to get a full script. Besides the director and the main actors, no one touches a full-length script. The honchos just won't tolerate it."

Slye nodded, listening intently.

"So we started to narrow it down. There were only a few folks who knew you auditioned for that role. The producer, director, and your main competition, Wyatt Woodside."

Ford picked up the explanation. "We ruled Wyatt out after confronting him. So that narrowed it down to just another pair of folks."

"You already told us you let it slip to Arthur Woolsey that you had been offered a contract from Republic Pictures." Jimmy continued. "We saw you arguing with the station manager yesterday morning and assumed there was some tension. That's why we devised a plan for Myra Ellington to audition for Woolsey in private."

"Not an easy task," Ford noted. "While I was rifling through Woolsey's private library, Myra was grilling old man Woolsey about Mr. Slye."

Leonard Slye perked up at the mention of his name.

"Did you know Arthur Woolsey had offered to give your band a reduced schedule so you could pursue your movie career?" Jimmy asked the handsome cowboy.

"How's that again?" Slye questioned. He turned to his agent, Jerry North. "You told us Woolsey wouldn't let us out of that contract!"

The agent's face flushed. He turned a sheet of white.

"Yes, Mr. North, explain that," Ford continued. "Actually, never mind, I'll explain it." He unfurled a document from his breast pocket and handed it to Leonard Slye. "I confiscated this from Woolsey's desk while he was chasing Myra around."

Slye studied the document, a frown revealing his emotions. "This is a fair deal! The money would be less, but my hourly burden would decrease and I could begin filming."

"That's what I thought," Ford said. "So I asked myself, why would Jerry North turn down that offer? I mean, he had you under contract as a movie star and a singing sensation. Why wouldn't he want to negotiate your release from Woolsey's regiment?"

The burly investigator poked a taut finger at Jerry North.

"Are you going to tell him or should we?"

Jerry North was perspiring. His coolness had evaporated under the cross-examination of Ford and Jimmy. He tried one last attempt at deception.

"Are you going to listen to this drivel, Leonard? These men are grasping at straws. They don't know what happened to that script!"

Ford nodded his manner calm.

"Absolutely, correct, yet you must admit, you're the only other person who had knowledge of the script being in Leonard's possession. You're the only one who knew he was stopping for a bite." He bared his teeth. "Why'd you take it?"

North was flustered. "I didn't…I mean…"

Leonard Slye intervened. "Jerry, this opportunity means so much for my career. Tell me the truth and I'll try to keep you out of it. Believe me, I don't want that kind of publicity."

Jerry North began to sob.

"I'm so sorry, Leonard. I didn't mean to ruin you. We had a good thing going with the Sons. You guys were making dough in the radio business, and I just thought to myself, why ruin a good thing? I figured I could setup another one of my actors with the script, make a few changes, and sell it to the competition." His face twisted with sorrow. "It's not like you and the boys would go hungry. I mean, sooner or later, you would have broken through to stardom. You're just too talented to keep grounded."

Leonard Slye absorbed the confession with a moment of silence.

"Is it too late? Did you already sell the script?"

North shook his head vigorously. "No, no, not at all!"

Jimmy McGee unlocked the office door. He left it open and departed. Rutherford Jones turned and addressed Leonard Slye.

"If you wish to get the police involved, we can arrange it, but something tells me it won't be necessary."

Leonard Slye shook the big man's hand.

"If Jerry returns the script and squares us with Arthur Woolsey, all will be forgiven." He stared at the hunched form of Jerry North, sobbing in the corner. "After this, I may not want to further my movie career."

Ford slapped him on the back. "Don't even ponder it, Mr. Slye. You see an opportunity, you pull the trigger."

Slye brightened up. "Say, I like that! Even though I want to be a big screen cowboy, I've never been fond of guns. Maybe someday I'll put that word trigger to a better use?"

"You could always give your dog that name?"

"Maybe I will."

THE END

EXPANSION

Oakland 1936

Myra Ellington slammed the door as hard as she could.
"Damn you, Rutherford!"

Jimmy McGee, who was sitting casually at his desk, nursing cheap hooch from a flask, jumped out of his chair.

"That's my cue to scram." The gaunt youth twisted the cap back on his vim before bolting from the chair.

Myra Ellington wasn't deterred. "Where is he, Jimmy? Where is that good for nothing devil?"

From the back room emerged a gigantic dark, muscular man.

"Hush your cursing woman! This is a place of business."

Myra glared wildly at Ford. "Don't you sass me, you big lug! I could strangle you right now."

Ford Jones sought help from his assistant, Jimmy, but the frail youth had already exited to the safety of the first floor.

"Listen, honey, whatever is eating you, we can…" Ford began.

This only incensed the woman further. "You barbarian! You did it again!" She aimed a sharp fingernail in his direction. "This is the third job you cost me this month!"

Ford displayed a look of ignorance. "What are you jabbering about?"

"Don't you take that tone with me, Rutherford Jones! You just can't help yourself, can you? Everything was going so well. I was going to open up for the main act next week!"

Myra was a lounge singer, a good one, albeit, a suddenly unemployed one.

"Look, baby, I'm sorry," Ford confessed. "It just happened."

An incredulous look draped over Myra Ellington's usually pleasant face. "It just happened? Ford, they told me you knocked out the owner and two of his employees. How does that just happen?"

The burly investigator shrugged. "I don't know. It just did." He paused and cringed. "Again. Look, I'll admit I might have been a little short fused, but…"

"Short fused? You broke the man's nose, Ford! And his goons are at the dentist."

91

Ford couldn't contain his grin. "Is that so?"

A menacing glare from the coffee colored siren wiped the joy from his face.

"Ford, how am I ever going to move out of that whack job's apartment, if you keep making me lose my job?"

Rutherford Jones rushed over to the door and peeked outside. "Shhh. She might hear you."

"Like I care!" The words dripped like venom from the curvaceous woman. "That pebble dealing fraud does nothing but treat us like servants anyway!"

Ford gave her a warning glance. "Enough, Myra. Linda Mae has issues I'll admit, but she has done a world of good for you. What white woman would take in a penniless black lounge singer in these times?" He grabbed the angry girl and peered into her chocolate eyes. "She's eccentric but harmless."

Myra could tell when she had pushed the issue to its limits. She sighed and picked up the flask Jimmy McGee had left behind. She unscrewed the cap, thought about taking a sip, and changed her mind.

"That junk might make you go blind," he cautioned. "I don't know where Jimmy gets his booze from but there's a reason it comes cheap."

"He sure did scoot out of here like a jack rabbit," the girl noted.

"Do you blame him?"

Myra banged on the wall hard. "It's okay to return Jimmy."

She heard footfalls from the stairway. The feet hesitated at the unopened door.

"Did you kill him?" The skinny youth inquired, opening the door.

Myra tossed him his flask. "No, he smooth-talked his way out of it... again."

Jimmy McGee gulped a quick draw from the vim. "Yes, he does have a smooth tongue."

Ford looked annoyed. "Too bad I can't use it." He pointed to the door. Jimmy had stenciled some letters the week before. It read: Rutherford Jones, Private Investigator.

Jimmy sighed. "It is what it is."

They were referring to their unique situation. Ford had long ago figured out that his clientele were not going to be swayed by hiring a black private eye, so he had developed a clever guise. He decided to hire his friend, Jimmy McGee, a young white Irishman, to pose as the company's figure head. Jimmy had adopted Ford's identity and had rechristened Ford, as Rufus, the black assistant.

The ploy had worked well. Jimmy interviewed prospective clients, whereas Ford actually did the investigative work. Only Myra knew the truth. Even Jimmy's girlfriend, Linda Mae, was unaware that Rufus the handyman was actually Rutherford Jones. She had assumed Jimmy wanted to distance himself from his Gaelic heritage.

Just then, Linda Mae, the owner of the second-hand jewelry shop, poked her head into the office.

The so-called office also served as the two men's apartment. Inside the utility closet were two folding cots which served as beds when the sun went down.

"What's all this fracas I hear?" demanded the zany blonde. She was a good ten years older than Jimmy, but the youth was still smitten by her.

"Hey, doll!" the frail youth piped in, removing his bowler. "The kids were having a discussion."

Linda Mae strutted around the office with an air of arrogance. "These people. They can't carry a normal conversation without breaking the sound barrier."

Myra's face contorted with anger. "These people?"

Linda Mae ignored the remark. "Poor girl. I heard you lost your job again. Such a shame, a real pity with that sweet voice you possess, but I can't say I'm surprised. Your attitude needs adjusting."

"What the hell is that supposed to mean?" demanded the sultry siren.

Jimmy gulped down another swig of the rotgut. He had seen this show before. The two girls would begin to engage in contemptuous banter until the men put an end to it, usually with the promise of wallet hurting gifts.

"Girls, please!" the Irishman began, but Myra wouldn't have it.

"No, Jimmy, I want to hear what this glass stone seller wants to say."

Linda Mae snorted. "Really, dear, mocking my profession. I'll have you know I am a reputable gem dealer, and I have an impeccable reputation." She snarled and turned up her nose. "I have been employed steadily these last five years, not a small feat in these dreadful economic times."

"If by employed you mean buying people's possessions at dirt cheap prices and hawking them to suckers, I'll dispute your claim of nobility."

Linda Mae was not unruffled. "Just the kind of remark I'd expect from a frustrated artist."

"Oh no, you didn't!"

Rutherford Jones had heard enough. "Please, you two, Jimmy and I will be late for our appointment if you don't leave us to get ready."

Linda Mae stared at him with apprehension. "Rufus, I'm sure you mean well and your loyalty to my Jimmy is admirable, but I don't appreciate you taking that tone with me."

"Sorry, ma'am," Ford immediately sputtered.

Jimmy could see that Myra was about to flip her lid, so he begrudgingly reached into his billfold. "You ladies are forgetting that today is Tuesday."

"What?" both girls echoed.

Ford came to life. "That's right, ladies. Carvers' truck was pulling in when I was washing the car out front. Looked to me like it was fully loaded."

Both girls' eyes lit up.

Carvers was their favorite dress shop, and on Tuesdays he restocked his inventory. Ford and Jimmy had done him a favor in negotiating with some loan sharks awhile back and the dress dealer was still grateful.

The skinny youth handed each of the girls a wad of money. "Go over and remind old man Carver he owes me. He'll knock off a few dollars for you."

Myra's eyes shone bright. There was nothing the voluptuous songstress enjoyed better than buying a new outfit. A glow enveloped her attractive features. "Thanks, Jimmy. Maybe this will help me as I begin auditioning all over again."

Linda Mae couldn't help herself. "Really Jimmy, you should be more cautious the way you hand money over. I mean, Rufus, he works hard for it, but this girl, she…"

Jimmy handed her another few bills. "Stop by O'Hara's and get us a bottle, my dear. Champagne, this time."

The daffy blonde swooned. "Oh, Jimmy!"

"Oh, brother!" Myra Moaned. "Let's go, miss prim and proper before they run out of our sizes."

Linda Mae's joy turned sour again. "The way you squeeze your assets into a gown, you'll make any size fit."

"Why, I oughta…" Myra protested.

Rutherford Jones didn't hear the rest. He had quietly backpedaled into the adjacent room, stranding his frail partner with the quarreling pair.

"Wait for me, big guy! Don't leave me with these two sharks!"

• • •

Ford squeezed the sedan into a narrow alleyway secreted behind Wu Chiong's Chinese restaurant.

"Why are we parking here?" asked Jimmy.

Ford turned his thick neck toward the back seat. "Seriously? This is Wu Chiong we are talking about."

Wu Chiong was the wizened leader of the Nine Blades, a ruthless Asian mob in charge of Oakland's Chinese underground.

"Right, boss."

"Don't call me that in front of Chiong's men. Wu's a crafty old fox, but his lackeys don't know how our operation works."

Jimmy nodded in agreement. "What do you think the old bag of bones wants now?"

Ford shrugged. "Can't imagine, but his voice sounded concerned."

"Old Leatherface showed emotion?"

They spied a couple of chefs smoking cigarettes near the back door of Chiong's lair. The cooks glared suspiciously at Ford before tossing their butts to the ground. Hastily, they retreated inside.

"Well, now they know we're here," Ford said exiting the vehicle.

Neither man felt particularly confident entering the premises. They had limited experience dealing with the iron-fisted ruler of the Nine Blades. Although, the elderly leader had dealt fairly with them, somehow he always managed to come out on top of the situation. Ford supposed they should feel blessed just for surviving each encounter.

Lately, the two men had come to a mutual agreement with the crusty old mobster. They would keep out of his business in exchange for Chiong's valuable input. The Chinese seemed to have a pipeline into all underworld activity. So far the arrangement had been very profitable to both parties.

"I swear if that old bag starts disrespecting me again…" Jimmy began.

"You'll do nothing," Ford answered. "We've invested too much in our partnership with the Chinese. Don't start mouthing off."

Jimmy feigned a look of innocence. "Me? Mouth off? Heaven forbid."

The skinny youth allowed Ford to open the restaurant door for him. It was early evening, and business was slow. Then again, business always seemed slow. Who could afford to dine out? And those who could did not venture into the seedy parts of Chinatown.

One of Chiong's men spotted the two. He simply nodded and pointed to the stairway. That indicated they were expected.

"Thankee very muchee," Jimmy mocked, arousing a groan from Ford.

The mobster remained stoic, ignoring the barb. He carefully retrieved a pen knife from his pocket and casually picked at his fingernails.

"Hope that's not our dinnerware?" Jimmy tossed snidely.

Rutherford Jones grabbed his partner roughly and yanked him up the stairway two at a time. They reached the top quickly. Standing in front of the doorway was Denny, Chiong's number one, and future successor. The young Asian glared at the pair.

"Ford Jones and his pet to see you, sir," the mobster spat.

Jimmy inched close to the man, sniffing him wildly. "Saints alive, boy! I thought you people were experts at laundry?"

Denny ignored the frail youth and frisked him roughly.

"Did you enjoy that?" Jimmy teased. "I haven't felt soft hands like that since I went down to the peep show last year."

Ford brushed his partner aside and assumed the position for his patdown. He knew Denny respected him. He also knew Denny feared him.

"Ford." The Asian stated in a monotone voice.

"Denny."

Denny opened the office door and waved them. "They're clean sir."

"Can't say the same about your hired help," Jimmy shouted as he barreled through the doorway.

Wu Chiong was seated at his desk, his chair facing out the window so that his back was turned to the pair.

Ford could see the wrinkled neck of the Nine Blades leader crimp up at the sound of Jimmy's voice.

"Come in, Mister Jones," the rubber skinned leader muttered. He spun his chair and faced the pair. "I've been waiting patiently."

Ford greeted the man with a firm handshake. Despite his age and sickly appearance, he knew Chiong to be virile.

"And don't forget Mama Mcgee's boy," Jimmy babbled. "Why don't you have your tool, Denny, rustle up some of that cat urine you pass off as wine."

Wu Chiong briefly made eye contact with Jimmy before turning his attention to Ford. "Clearly, this man needs assistance. Who but a fool would describe our alcohol as cat urine, yet beg for it to be fetched?"

"Jimmy McGee don't beg for nothing!" Bottles blurted in anger.

The saggy old man bared his yellow teeth. "Quiet, drunken sod or I will have him serve you from the latrine!"

Ford suppressed a chuckle. "Begging your pardon, sir, but it was a hassle dragging ourselves away from clientele to meet up with you. Can you tell us what this is all about?"

Now it was Wu Chiong's turn to chuckle. "Surely, you jest, Rutherford. You have no clients waiting. You've had no clients for a couple of weeks now."

"How would you know that, you bag of bones?" Jimmy demanded. "Have you been spying on us?"

Chiong simply sighed. "This man weighs a hundred pounds and yet he refers to me as a bag of bones?"

"I tip the scale at a buck thirty!" Jimmy rifled off.

"Yes, most of it drenched with the vulgar booze your type likes to imbibe from."

Jimmy made a weird face of anger mixed with confusion. "I don't take bribes from anybody!"

Ford interrupted the bickering pair. "Mr. Chiong, you're correct, we are between cases right now. Do you have work for us?"

Chiong settled back in his chair comfortably. "Ah, that's what I wish to talk about." He gripped the arm of his chair and lifted himself to a standing position. Ford had to stop himself from grabbing the man's elbow.

"I am not a man of luxury." The Asian stated. He pointed to the window frame. It displayed a view of the brick building next door. "I keep a meager existence. Long ago, I came to the realization that material objects do not entertain me the way they did in my youth."

Jimmy began to say something, but a rough elbow from Ford made him choke back his comment.

The old man continued. "I run a small but successful business. It is no secret that I control the Oakland area and I am content in that knowledge."

Ford cleared his throat. "Why do I get the feeling you're about to give me some unpleasant news?"

Chiong stared at him in anger. "Has your dog's rudeness worn off on you?"

Jimmy ruffled at the barb. "Ford didn't mean to disrespect you, Wu. It's just at your age; you shouldn't be wasting your words on poetry. Just spill it. What do you want from us?"

Chiong sighed and sat back down in his chair, clearly upset. It was a side of the Nine Blades leader that Ford had never seen before. It sent a shiver down his spine. What news could so severely depress Wu Chiong?

"There have been rumblings from the other side of the bay," Chiong whispered.

"San Francisco?" Ford inquired.

The old man nodded. "A truly powerful clan. Many times the size of my own."

"What beef you have with those slants?" Jimmy mumbled.

Ford gave him a fierce glare. "What Jimmy means, sir, is why would they bother with you? Chinese don't battle Chinese."

"Normally, I would agree, Mr. Jones, but there has been a lot of chatter."

"Chatter?"

"My men keep ears everywhere. There have been rumblings of a takeover in San Francisco's Chinatown. I can't verify if it is true. But if there is any truth to the rumor, my connection with Warren Lee will be broken."

Warren Lee was the undisputed ruler of San Francisco's Chinese underworld. No one knew his real name. He had adopted Warren a few years back. Jimmy had joked that he meant to take Warner as name, but no one could verify.

"So why don't you just reach out to Lee?" Ford asked.

Chiong trembled. "I have. I sent a man last week."

Jimmy raised an eyebrow. "I don't like where this is heading."

"What happened to your courier, Mr. Chiong?" Ford begged.

Chiong curled his gnarly hands and reached into his desk drawer. He moved slowly and deliberately. When he was done fishing around in the drawer, he plucked an item and deposited it on the wooden desk.

The item thumped loudly as it clattered on the surface.

"Saints alive!" screamed Jimmy.

"Holy crap!" Ford muttered.

The object of their shock and awe was a severed hand. It lay lifeless on the table, its ring finger still adorned with an opal stone.

"This is what is left of Denny's cousin," Chiong announced.

For once, Jimmy was speechless, not out of remorse for Denny's loss, but out of a sense of dread.

"You slants don't mess around!"

Chiong made an effort to rise from his chair again.

"Mr. McGee," he stated quietly. It was the first time he had ever addressed Jimmy by his last name. "I've tolerated your rudeness and sarcasm for quite some time, but I will not have you use that vile expression in my presence any further. Am I clear?"

Jimmy waited a moment, measuring the old man's words before he slumped apologetically. "Yes, Wu, I have crossed the line. " He removed his bowler. "That disgusting word will not escape my lips any longer."

"But it will remain unspoken?" Chiong managed a smile. He stared at Ford. "You can relate to ugly words I'm sure?"

"That goes without saying." Ford pointed at the severed hand. "I take it this is why I'm here?"

Chiong nodded, his long fingernails scraping the table.

"You want us to find out what happened?" Jimmy mumbled.

The wizened Asian managed a toothy grin. "It is obvious what happened. I want you two to find out what the future beholds."

Ford shook his head. "I'm not comfortable with taking on the Frisco gang."

Wu Chiong bristled. "No one has suggested any such action. I simply want you to investigate the situation. Find out what is going on. I need to know if Warren Lee is behind this heinous act or if he has been supplanted."

The veins on Ford's neck bulged out.

"You still hesitate, Mr. Jones?" Chiong reached back into the drawer and withdrew a small laundry bag. He unceremoniously hurled it at Jimmy.

Bottles McGee caught the bag in mid- air and peered at its contents. He exhaled a loud whistle.

"That's a lot of moolah!" the Irishman proclaimed, holding out the bag so Ford could take a look.

Ford tried to hide his excitement, but couldn't maintain his composure. "If we accept, and I mean, if, it will be on my terms."

Chiong grinned, knowing he had already reeled in his fish. "Of course, Mr. Jones."

Ford began pacing around the small office. "This will be an exploratory excursion."

"Agreed. Simply return with facts."

Jimmy tugged at his bowler. "What if the heat gets turned up?"

Chiong stared at the frail youth. "Your slang bewilders me. "

Ford clarified. "What Jimmy means, is, what happens if all hell breaks loose?"

Chiong's eyes narrowed. "Then you should be content knowing you have the backing of the Nine Blades."

Jimmy gulped. "I feel like I got nine blades already, all stuck in my back." He studied the contents of the laundry bag again.

Chiong wiggled a shaky finger at him. "That bag represents a goodwill gesture between us. If you gentlemen bring me back useful information, I assure you there will be many such gifts bestowed on you."

Ford offered a firm handshake. "I don't want to pick sides in a battle between Chinese warlords, but you know the old saying, the devil you know…"

•   •   •

The lights were still on when Ford and Bottles McGee returned to their decrepit office. Ford decided to check on the two girls first. Much to his chagrin, they were both sleeping peacefully on the plaid sofa, arm in arm. On the coffee table, lay several bags and boxes from Carver's Department Store, The soft tissue paper hiding the overpriced goodies the women had swooped up.

Ford helped himself to a handful of popcorn that rested by the radio. The device was still on, piping out melodious tunes. The girls were oblivious to the sound, their eyes blinking restlessly under the lids, suggesting they were experiencing deep, dream-filled sleep.

"That's a relief," Ford whispered.

For a few months now, Myra had lived downstairs in the jewelry shop with Linda Mae. It had made their relationship even more difficult. Two women could not live in harmony, especially when both were pampered, but looking at the pair now, Ford couldn't imagine them being any closer.

"Boy, I wish I had my camera for this!" Jimmy marveled.

The two girls lay side by side, grins a mile wide.

"You have to stop handing out our money!" Ford barked, almost waking the girls. "Look at those boxes! Old man Carver must have closed shop early tonight."

Jimmy stared at the scattered boxes. "I'll say." He scampered over to the fridge and peered inside. Linda Mae had remembered the champagne. "Some other night."

Ford turned off the radio and kissed Myra's forehead.

Even though the windows were closed, it was November and the winds had started to reel in the cool air from the bay. California Winter was on its way.

"Let's get out of here while the going is good," Jimmy suggested.

Ford nodded. He pulled down the light quilt from the back of the sofa and draped it over the sleeping women. Jimmy then flicked off the light as the two men headed up the stairway to their own apartment.

Ford strained his huge muscles as he pushed the desk up against the wall and deposited the two chairs on top of it. While he did that, Jimmy extracted the two cots from the hall closet and unfolded them. Within seconds they had set up their sleeping quarters.

Jimmy gripped the laundry bag filled with money.

"What should I do with this, Ford?"

The dark skinned warrior stretched his arms and shrugged, "Beats me. It's not safe here. We'll take it down to the bank in the morning, but for now it's best we keep it as close as possible."

"…the old saying, the devil you know."

"Say no more." The skinny Irishman replied. He tossed the bag on top of his cot, threw his bowler across the room, and plunged his weary limbs down on the bed. "This is the safest place, bub. They'd have to cut my head off to get it."

Ford grimaced. "Did you have to say that?"

Jimmy gulped. A drastic vision of the severed hand crossed his mind.

"These Chinese don't mess around. Wu's a tough old bird, but I could see his bones were rattled."

"I agree."

"So how do we expect to succeed where his messengers failed?"

Ford yanked off his loafers and unbuttoned his shirt. "Beats me, Jimmy. We've been very lucky in our encounters with Wu Chiong and the Nine Blades, but from what I hear, they're infants compared to the San Francisco clan."

Jimmy raised his head from the laundry bag. "Warren Lee has a nasty reputation. I hear even the politicians play nice with him."

"We can't be sure Warren sent that severed hand to Chiong. They've never had issues before, and the Chinese are notoriously loyal to each other."

"You driving at something?"

Ford groaned. "Nope, just thinking out loud, Jimmy." He stretched out on the cot. He didn't bother with a blanket. "Wu Chiong is a man of mystery. We can never take anything he says at face value. "

"Right."

"First and foremost, he's a businessman. Oakland is a nice slice of the pie, but it's still only a slice."

Jimmy sat up. "And sometimes, the urge for a second helping is mighty powerful."

Ford winked. "You're getting good at this craft, Mr. McGee."

"You, too, Rutherford Jones."

Moments later, both men were snoring, refueling their bodies for the perils that lay ahead.

*   *   *

The initial footfalls didn't wake them. It was the creaky door that alerted Ford to the intruders. His weary eyes opened just in time to see a dark clad man rushing toward him. The attacker had a metal pipe in his hand.

Instinctively, Ford rolled off his cot onto the floor. It was a good thing his reflexes were fast, as the black suited figure slammed the pipe down where Ford's head had rested seconds ago.

A second figure rushed through the doorway. The need for stealth had disappeared. Ford was aware of their presence as he sprung to his feet in a crouching gesture.

"Jimmy! Get up!"

Usually, Jimmy McGee would be in a drunken slumber by now, sleeping off a bottle of rotgut, but because of his visit to Wu Chiong's restaurant, Jimmy had remained sober this evening. That lone fact had probably saved his life.

"Huh? What?" He muttered in a groggy tone.

The second intruder was only inches away from the bony youth, his metal pipe gleaming in the pale moonlight that peeked through the office blinds.

Rutherford Jones darted across the room, his old baseball speed kicking in. He had been a pitcher for the Detroit Wolves in their only year of existence, but even pitchers took part in the daily sprints. Ford was fast, very fast.

His right fist connected harshly with the much smaller figure, causing him to stumble forward and fall over Jimmy's cot. Jimmy reacted instinctively, hammering the mask ridden intruder on the back of his neck.

While this was happening, the other black-clad man had made a mad dash for the laundry bag. He had one hand on it when Ford tackled him chest high. Both men barreled into the wall, knocking out plaster.

"That's it Ford! Whack that creep!" Jimmy bellowed, sitting on top of the other man.

Ford's momentum had knocked the wind out of the smaller man. More importantly, it had dislodged the metal pipe. It clanged to the floor harmlessly.

Ford jabbed a quick left at the masked man, but much to his dismay, the smaller figure dodged it easily and struck out at Ford with an open palm.

Much to his shock, Ford was sent sprawling backward into the wall, his head striking it hard. He saw stars for a moment as he tried to shake the cobwebs from his skull. The smaller opponent seized the opportunity to further his attack. He peppered Ford with punches to the midsection, most notably the solar plexus.

Ford felt the air getting sucked out of his lungs. His knees began to buckle. His light-headedness had increased, and he felt himself losing the battle.

Desperately, the big man reached out and grabbed the smaller man in a bear hug. The masked intruder squirmed, trying to free himself from Ford's iron grasp.

"Stay still or I'll crush your ribs!" Ford hissed. He was serious, the anger seething from his lips.

The intruder ignored his warning and tried the only thing he could. He head butted Ford with all his strength. The impact was ferocious. Both skulls collided in a deafening thud.

Ford felt his arms go numb as he was forced to release his grip. A trickle of blood poured into his eyes and he knew his skin had been busted open. He staggered back.

The other man didn't fare much better. He, too, was severely wounded by the blow. The man wobbled back, seeking his metal pipe to end the conflict.

He needn't bother. Bottles McGee had retrieved the weapon. The frightened Irishman waved it menacingly.

'Don't make me use this!" He threatened.

The black-clad attacker simply bowed in a sign of obedience. Jimmy was flustered.

"What gives?"

Ford had regained some bit of composure. He was pointing behind Jimmy frantically. Jimmy wheeled just in time to see the other man exiting the office, laundry bag in hand.

"Oh hell!" Bottles McGee howled, turning to give chase.

He had barely made it to the doorway when he heard a rumbling sound. It was the attacker making his way down the stairway. Only, he wasn't walking. He was sliding on his back, his eyes closed. Jimmy watched as the man's body dragged its way along each stair, finally slumping to the bottom.

"Well, I'll be damned!" The skinny Irishman cursed.

"No, that guy will be damned!"

The voice emanated from the lovely mouth of Myra Ellington, standing gloriously in the shadows, clad only in the thinnest of negligees, the moonlight shining enough to give Jimmy a full view of her magnificent assets.

Oddly enough, Jimmy McGee was able to avert his gaze from her heaving breasts, as his eyes focused on her arms. In them, lay a baseball bat, a souvenir from Ford's playing days.

"Woman, you are a sight for sore eyes!" Jimmy proclaimed.

Myra grinned before snarling and kicking the intruder again. "Who's your friend? And where's Ford?"

Jimmy's face turned white. "Oh, god, Ford…"

The big black man emerged from the doorway, a limp body in his arms. Ruthlessly, he hurled the intruder down the stairway to land in a heap with his brethren.

"Thank goodness!" Myra exclaimed.

Ford wiped the streaming blood from his eyes. "Is that my baseball bat, girl? You better not have cracked it!"

Myra Ellington held the bat in both hands, her hips swiveled toward the intruders.

"Don't make me come up there and give you some medicine, Rutherford Jones. Now you're bringing your work home with you?"

Ford eyed her curvaceous form appreciatively. "You would have wowed the crowd, baby!"

Jimmy cleared his throat loudly. "If the mutual admiration society meeting is over, I'd like to find out who these two clowns are."

Ford raced down the stairs, his muscular calves regaining their strength. He yanked the black masks roughly from both men. Not surprisingly, both intruders were Asian.

"Warren Lee's boys?" Jimmy asked.

"Could be," Ford replied. "Or they could belong to the Nine Blades or some renegade clan."

Myra shook her head and handed Ford the bat. "I'm going back to bed. Clean up your mess."

Ford watched her shimmy down the hallway back to the safety of the jewelry store. He heard the latch bolt back as he turned his attention to the unconscious men.

"Jimmy, I'm not sure if it's safe to leave the girls here."

The skinny Irishman concurred. "It's obvious these burglars were after the laundry bag."

"That means word is already out."

Jimmy stared at Ford. He was even more frightened. "Or it means old man Wu Chiong is getting stingy and wanted to recuperate his investment before we even get started."

Ford rubbed a hand across his chin. "I have an idea."

"I hope it's a good one because right now we have two half-dead bodies in our hallway."

"Yes, we do, Jimmy." Ford reached into his pants pocket and tossed

Jimmy the car keys. "Rev up the sedan. We're going to take these boys for a ride."

Jimmy gulped. "We are?"

"Yep, these Chinese react better to visual stimulation. We need to send them a message."

"And what would that be?"

Ford reached down and lifted one of the men over his shoulder as if it was as easy as carrying a bath towel.

"I want both Wu Chiong and Warren Lee to know that Rutherford Jones doesn't scare easily."

• • •

Ford's original plan was to drop one of the intruders in the middle of downtown San Francisco, but he quickly scrapped that idea. The travel time from Oakland to the larger city would take too long, and the investigator wanted to make sure he'd be finished by daylight. That trip would soon be decreased once the Bay Bridge opened. The bridge was scheduled to open within a week, and once it was finished, drivers would have a clear access back and forth from Oakland to San Francisco.

The backup plan, however, was easily deployed.

"These guys weigh a ton for such small shrimps." Jimmy grunted, heaving the unconscious form of one of the prisoners from the back seat.

Ford chuckled loudly. It amused him that skinny Jimmy would refer to anyone as a shrimp.

"Just make sure you tie them together tightly with the fishing wire but make sure you don't cut their wrists."

Jimmy shrugged and proceeded to drag the limp form onto the grassy knoll. They had decided to deposit the two bodies in front of the flower garden at City Hall. This would surely cause a stir with the media and local politicians.

"Did you finish that sign like I asked you?" Inquired Ford.

Jimmy allowed the body he was dragging to hit the ground. It did not land gently.

"Now listen here, Ford Jones, it's two in the morning, and I'm tired. I scratched the sign like you asked."

Ford stared at him impatiently, all the time carrying a body over his shoulder in a fireman's carry. He dumped the beaten intruder next to his companion.

"It's not that I don't trust you, Jimmy, but…I don't trust you."

Jimmy McGee stalked over to the sedan and withdrew a cardboard sign he had lettered on the way over. He shoved it defiantly under Ford's nose.

"This is what you're grilling me over?"

Ford took the sign and patiently flipped it over. He stared at it for a few seconds before a sly grin enveloped his features.

"What is it?" Asked Jimmy.

"What did I ask you to write?"

Jimmy rubbed his chin. "You told me to put down the words: Don't mess with us, and that's what I scribbled down."

Ford took another gander at the sign. "Looks like you wrote donut mess with us. What's this?" he asked, pointing to the apostrophe.

"That's an apostrophe!"

Ford shook his head. "No, that looks like the letter U."

Jimmy McGee placed his hands on his hips and gave Ford a stern look. "Next time, do it yourself! I didn't sign up for the rough stuff."

Ford waved him away. "Forget it, let's just hurry up."

The pair worked quickly, positioning the two black-clad men up against the base of the wooden fence facing City Hall. Jimmy bound the two men together and placed the sign on the smaller man's lap. He rubbed his hands together in accomplishment.

"What do you hope to get out of this?"

Ford took a moment to reply, before answering. "I want the Chinese to know that my home is off limits. This will send them a warning that the next time, the bodies won't be returned."

Jimmy shuddered at the tone in Ford's voice. For the first time ever, he was scared of his employer.

"Let's scram, boss. I don't want to be around when the press gets ahold of this."

Ford nodded and laid a reassuring hand on his friend's shoulder.

"It's going to be OK, Jimmy."

The frail youth allowed his gaze to take in the pair of intruders one more time.

"That's what I keep telling myself, Ford." He started the car engine. "We've never been in it this deep before. Maybe we should send the girls away?"

Ford tried to keep positive. "If it comes to that, I have favors to call in. We'll get them a safe-house if things get darker."

Jimmy drove away. Usually, Ford did the driving, but his tiny partner took the initiative. Probably, for the best, Ford thought. Better to keep Jimmy's mind occupied. He was twenty-five and street wise, but still a dreamer who deserved his shot at a better life.

●   ●   ●

Myra Ellington slammed the morning paper on Ford's desk. The big man had still been snoozing. Startled, he almost rolled off the cot.

He rubbed the sand from his eyes and yawned.

"Good morning to you, too!"

"Don't you give me that good morning routine, Ford Jones!"

Myra's outburst revived Jimmy McGee from slumber-land.

"Saints alive!" The Irishman blurted. He was still dressed in his day wear.

Myra Ellington turned her barely clad body toward the toothpick thin man.

"That goes for you too, James McGee!"

Jimmy rubbed his eyes, hoping for a better look at her magnificent form. He peered intently at her heaving chest, threatening to burst through the thin negligee. He drank in her leggy profile.

"Easy, Jimmy, before your eyes pop out," Ford warned.

He staggered out of the cot to retrieve the news rag and discover what was causing his girlfriend's rant. His eyes widened as he caught a glance of the paper's headline: Turf War?

The headline was accompanied by a photo of the two black-clad intruders tied up and displaying Jimmy's hastily written sign.

"Those are the men I had to save you from last night!" Myra accused.

Ford cast her a raised eyebrow. He focused on the paragraph below the headline, which questioned why two Chinese men had been left outside City Hall. The reporter had guessed the mysterious underworld of Chinatown had suffered some sort of turbulence.

"Yep," Ford concluded, tossing the paper back at his woman.

"Aren't you chilly?" Jimmy asked, his eyes glued to her shapely form.

Myra ignored his barb. "You two better put this problem to rest…and soon. I don't want to have to deal with Linda Mae's anxiety."

Both men stared at each other with wide eyes.

"She slept through all that?" Jimmy wondered.

Myra nodded, her scowl still plastered across her face. "Bad enough she thinks the depression was caused by "negro aggression," her words, not mine."

Ford searched out for his pants and drew them on quickly.

"Look, Myra, I don't have time to go into what's happening, but it might be a good idea for you and Linda Mae to close up shop for a few days and head over to Los Angeles…just until Jimmy and I have sorted this affair out."

The beautiful girl started to frown, but her expression turned to one of dismay as she glimpsed the seriousness of Ford's expression.

"Maybe you're right. Maybe we should close down the jewelry shop for a couple of days."

"Why would we close down the jewelry shop?"

The voice belonged to Linda Mae. She stood wild-eyed, her hair straggling all over the place. She clutched at her bathrobe as she stood in the doorway of Ford's office.

"Baby, you're awake!" Jimmy McGee greeted with honest sincerity.

Linda Mae smiled briefly at her boyfriend before turning back to Myra.

"Well, Myra, explain yourself," she demanded. "And for heaven's sake, why must you parade around naked? "

Myra lifted her nose in the air.

"I'll have you know this is the latest style in night wear."

Jimmy flashed a grin. "I approve of it."

Linda Mae waved a warning finger at the young girl. "You see that? You corrupt an innocent like my Jimmy. That's why Rufus was able to kidnap you in the first place."

Rufus was the name Ford was known to by Linda Mae. She had no idea that he was the actual private eye and not Jimmy. She had fallen for the two men's tale immediately. It didn't seem a stretch to her that Jimmy would be the boss. She was blinded by her affection for him. It had struck her as quaint that he had hired Rufus as a handyman and treated him like a partner.

When Myra had entered her life, Linda Mae just assumed she was a victim of circumstances and she believed Ford treated the woman like a possession. Nothing could be further from the truth.

Jimmy cleared his throat. He did his best to smooth the wrinkles from his worn suit.

"Listen, Linda Mae, there was a problem here last night…"

She interrupted him. "Well, you honestly can't expect the man to behave when she prowls around dressed like that." She stared at Ford with disdain. "Really, Rufus, you must control your actions. This girl is not your property. She is a human being."

Myra expressed her gratitude. "Thank you, Linda Mae. That was really heartfelt."

Linda Mae refused to give her roommate the satisfaction. "Although, how a woman with so many fine dresses, always seems naked, I will never understand."

Ford laughed. "I believe Jimmy was talking about something else, Linda Mae."

The skinny youth grabbed her hands together, clasping them in his own.

"Someone broke in last night."

"Dear Lord! Did they take my jewels?"

Myra couldn't help but scoff.

"Even a petty crook could tell them pebbles is worthless costume jewelry."

Ford stepped between the two girls.

"Yes, Rufus?" Linda Mae questioned.

"We would feel safer if you two were secure over in Los Angeles for a couple of days."

Linda Mae studied the seriousness of his features. "Well, Rufus, that's truly kind of you, but totally unnecessary. Stores have been burglarized in Oakland for years now. Open your eyes, look around, there are hungry people. Desperate men will do desperate things. "

"Linda Mae..." Jimmy began.

This time, it was Myra who intervened.

"Can it Jimmy. The woman is right. She worked too hard to build up her business. No two-bit nightcrawlers are going to scare us away."

A stern frown flashed on Ford's face. He knew arguing was out of the question. Myra, alone, was a formidable challenge. Throw in Linda Mae, and the pair was unmatchable.

He studied Jimmy questioningly. The thin youth shrugged.

"Wasting our time?"

Jimmy nodded. "Without a doubt."

Linda Mae had snagged the blanket from Ford's cot. She draped it across Myra's shoulders.

"Cover yourself up, Myra."

Surprisingly, the songstress didn't refuse. She wrapped the blanket around her body and departed without a word. Even covered, her desirable form was inescapable.

Linda Mae turned her attention to Jimmy McGee.

"Is it serious, James?"

Jimmy peered at her eyes. They almost hid her fear, but he could detect a trace of it. It made him love her even more.

"Nah, doll, you were right, probably a couple of hungry guys."

The ditzy blonde shivered. "Let's hope so."

Rutherford Jones waited until after she had left before trolling over to his desk. Jimmy wondered if he sought the bottle of scotch he kept there. Ford had something more sinister in mind.

He withdrew his revolver and checked to make sure it was loaded. Of course it was. He had owned it for years, and was proud of the fact that he had never fired it.

"You think we'll need that?" Jimmy asked dryly.

Ford ignored his gaze. Instead, he withdrew the remainder of his ammunition.

"I hope to never use this, Jimmy, but…"

"But this is unknown territory," his partner finished.

•   •   •

After a quick shower and breakfast with the women, Ford and Jimmy headed out for the day. Their first stop was the bank. It wasn't very crowded this early in the morning. Then again, lately, it was never very crowded.

Ford felt a great burden lifted from his shoulders when the cash was deposited. Jimmy tossed the soiled laundry bag into the trash. He didn't want it as a keepsake to remind him of last night's adventure. Within seconds, one of the needy denizens scooped up the deserted bag and clutched it like they had just panned gold.

"Let's get out of here." Ford quipped, anxious to begin the trail.

They had devised a simple plan; head to San Francisco's Chinatown and accomplish two things. First, make sure Warren Lee was still the kingpin. Second, confirm that the message to the Nine Blades did originate from his core of thieves.

Ford found a parking spot not too far from the Oakland pier.

In 1868, Central Pacific Rail Road had created the magnificent waterfront empire known as Oakland Long Wharf. From there you could board a ferry for the short trip to San Francisco, where you would get off at the San Francisco Ferry building.

Until the massive Bay Bridge would open in a few days, this was how people got across the watery bay. As such, it was a thriving mecca for business. The pier was the brainchild of Francis M. Smith, who had envisioned the need for travel between the two cities. He had devised this plan, named the Key Route, and its focal center was a 17,000-foot pier.

The pier was also home to various storage yards for coal and lumber. Each day, over a quarter million travelers ventured across the water on nearly three hundred separate departures. It was an economic boon in a rather blighted area. This would all likely vanish once the wonder project, known as the Bay Bridge would be unveiled. The city was already planning a jubilant grand opening.

"Should I grab a couple of tickets, boss?" Jimmy inquired.

Ford pondered his options. "Let's scout out the pier first, Jimmy. You know how long these trips last, and I'm anxious to put this to bed."

Jimmy nodded in agreement.

Although the distance itself between the two cities was minimal, the Southern Pacific was determined to drain as much cash from its customers as possible. The corporation was ruthless. Their solution was brilliant. The ferry liners crawled through the choppy waters at a snail's pace, making the trip interminable. As a result, voyagers were forced to endure a long ride. This led to boredom and hunger, which in turn led to commercialism.

The massive ferries were filled with shops and dining rooms, all eager to stake a claim.

Ford hated that the government allowed this monopoly to continue. He was the first to applaud years back when the Bay Bridge construction was announced. Yes, a passenger would still be forced to shill over their hard earned money on tolls, but at least the trip would be shorter and in the privacy of your own vehicle.

"You two gents look like men who are in a hurry."

The voice emanated from a colorfully dressed man in a bright blue outfit. The man was a bit chubby, but it made him seem friendlier. He wore a vest over his shirt that was adorned with buttons of nautical design.

"Ferry trip too long? Why don't you try a private ride?"

Ford stared at the man's neatly written sign.

"Wharf Charters?"

The chubby man gripped Ford's hand and pulled him closer.

"That's right big man, and today is your lucky day!"

"How so?" asked Jimmy McGee.

The man sucked in a mouthful of air. "Don't spread the word, but business has been tough." He pointed to the Bay Bridge in the shadows of the wharf. "Looks like a big dragon if you ask me."

"You mentioned something about luck?" said Ford.

"Yes, of course. You see, that monstrosity will open this weekend, and with it will go my business, and thus my income. My wife hasn't told the children yet, but they are young and healthy. We will endure."

"Sorry, mister," said Jimmy. "That's some tough apples to swallow."

The chubby man nodded in agreement. "Alas, my loss will be your gain."

"How so?" Jimmy repeated.

"Today only, is buy one, get one day. And the best part is it's the same fee you would pay to be on the Garden City."

The Garden City was the name of the biggest ferry departing from Oakland Wharf. Ford had ridden it multiple times. He knew it was like a floating town, the crew churning the paddle wheels ever so slightly. He had once joked that he had celebrated a birthday during the unending trip.

"Did I mention that we go top speed?" the jolly man whispered. "Fastest ship in the port, and only enough room for ten passengers."

Ford looked at Jimmy. The skinny youth nodded.

"Ok, mister, we'll take you up on the offer."

The chubby man beamed with satisfaction. "That'll be two bits, men."

Jimmy pulled the coins from his coat pocket and handed them over.

"And the tickets?" the frail youth piped up.

The big man chuckled. "No need, you see my sign." He pointed down at the beginning of the pier. "See that small ship? That's mine. They're waiting for you guys."

Jimmy squinted at the end of the dock. He saw an old timer undoing the ropes that held the small tug at bay.

"Better hurry up gents. He's getting ready to cast off. Here, let me let him know you're coming."

He raised a hand and waved frantically to the old man. The elderly sailor stared back and then waved in confirmation.

The chubby salesman checked a pocket watch. It looked expensive.

"You got two minutes to catch it or you're going to have to wait for the next trip."

Ford yanked Jimmy by the arm. "Let's go kid. I want to reach Chinatown as quickly as possible."

Jimmy was already ahead of him as they sprinted down the boardwalk. Halfway down, Ford started shouting to the elderly sailor. "Hold that boat!"

The wrinkled sailor heard their pleas and held his rope firmly.

"Who you yelling at boy? "

The angry sailor jabbed a finger in Jimmy's direction. "You better have that darkie zip his trap."

Jimmy caught his breath before yelling. "We wanted to make sure you didn't leave without us."

The old sailor shot him a queer look.

"Now why the heck would I be taking on you two boys?"

Ford wasn't even winded from the sprint.

"Wharf Charters, right?"

The sailor nodded. "Aye, that's the business name."

Jimmy relaxed. "We just paid your fella two bits so you can take us across the bay."

"My fella?"

"Yeah, fat guy in a bright outfit. Right over there." Jimmy wheeled in the direction of the chubby huckster.

Only, he wasn't there any longer.

"Damn!" Ford cursed.

The sailor spit into the water. "That negro has a foul mouth on him."

Jimmy ignored the comment. "He's gone! He said you would be faster than the Garden City."

"Well, that's for sure. Who wouldn't be?"

Ford groaned. "Only, you're not taking passengers, are you?"

The grumpy sailor snorted. "You two just got scammed!"

"We did?" Jimmy begged.

The old man chuckled. "How old are you son? Thirty? Thirty-five?"

"I'm twenty-five, sir."

The sailor studied him. "You don't seem the foolish type. You chumps got hooked into an old con. It's been taking place since the first nails were driven into boats."

Jimmy's shoulders sagged. "So you're not taking us?"

"I didn't say that. Just not taking you for free."

"We just dropped two bits for nothing." Jimmy moaned.

Ford sized up the sailor. "How much do you want?"

The elderly man was taken aback. He glared at Ford with anger and then jabbed Jimmy with a rough elbow.

"Ornery darkie, that one is."

"," Jimmy began, "We really need to cross the bay right now. Can you help us out?"

The sailor remained quiet for what seemed like an eternity before he finally barked. "Five dollars will do it."

Ford's face drained of color, "Five dollars?"

"Each," the old man confirmed.

Jimmy shrugged and withdrew a sawbuck from his billfold. "You sir, are a criminal."

The elderly man saluted them with a crooked grin. "God bless America!"

Without another word, he unraveled the holding line and pushed off the dock. "Don't just stand there, dummies! Jump aboard!"

Ford and Jimmy heaved their frames onto the tugboat before it inched away from the mooring.

"If I ever get my hands on that porker, I'll ring his neck." Jimmy cursed.

Ford said nothing. He simply relaxed and tried to get some rest. He had a feeling he would need all his energy to combat whatever lay in wait.

•   •   •

The voyage across the bay flew by without incident. The cranky old sailor remained silent, numb to his passengers while Ford and Jimmy passed the time debating over how they would spend the upcoming weekend.

Jimmy mentioned that Linda Mae had begged him to take her to see the new Disney film about the princess and her dwarves. The skinny youth had scoffed at the idea. A self-proclaimed movie fanatic, Jimmy wagered that America wasn't ready for a full-length animated feature, no matter how strong the buzz was.

Ford had other prospects in mind. Tommy Dorsey was making a stop in Los Angeles, and Myra made no secret about her desire to attend the show. The burly private investigator wasn't thrilled about spending an evening hobnobbing with the high-brow clientele, but his recent activities had caused the siren to lose yet another employment opportunity, and he felt an obligation to make it up to her. Besides, no one could resist the upbeat tempo of Dorsey's band.

When they had departed the tugboat, the crusty old seaman had grumbled something about a tip. Ford only chuckled, but Jimmy winked and mentioned he had left one in the toilet. The venomous old timer simply cursed and spat a wad of chewing gum into the water.

Within a matter of seconds, the pair were approached by a shady character.

"Excuse me, gents?"

"Yes?" Jimmy took the bait.

The man displayed two orange ferry tickets. "I have two weekly passes here, and I just got canned from the lumber yard. Can you see fit to take them off my hands?"

"I don't think so," Ford muttered.

"Please! I'm starving here!" the man whined.

Jimmy didn't hesitate, "How much, bub?"

Before the man could answer, Rutherford Jones had collared his pal by the neck and dragged him away from the crowded pier. Jimmy resisted for a brief second but realized he was probably about to get fleeced.

"Thanks, Ford. Guess I work better when I have a few belts under me. Let's say we hit a bar. I'm parched."

Ford saw that Jimmy had the shakes. This wasn't unusual in drunks.

"I'm inclined to say no, but I think you may have a point. I could use a little liquid courage myself, but just one."

"Agreed."

They stopped at the pier for an overpriced glass of stale beer before hailing a cab to Chinatown.

Oakland's Chinatown was the runt of the litter compared to the vast sprawling area known as San Francisco Chinatown. It, of course, was the largest concentration of Chinese Americans in the country.

"This is incredible!" Jimmy ejaculated.

He was peering at the assembly of nightclubs that had just popped up in the last year or two. There was the Forbidden City, the Skyroom, Club Mandalay, Kubla Khan, the Lion's Den and many more all resembling ancient Chinese structures of pagoda roofs and brightly colored lanterns.

"Once that bridge opens next week, this place will be flooded with tourists," Ford noted, taking in the marvelous view. "I expect the Hollywood types to make their way over."

"You think?"

The dark skinned muscle man nodded affirmatively. "It's a destination place. All you have to do is build, and the customers will come."

"And you think Warren Lee has his hands on the action?"

"Let me tell you, Jimmy. It doesn't matter what culture you come from. Black, white or Chinese. Money centers around politicians and gangsters. It's a fact."

Jimmy waved an arm at the bustling foot traffic.

"Sometimes that ain't a bad thing, boss."

It didn't take long to get noticed. A couple of Chinese men approached them from the side. The men wore red bandanas, rather than straw hats. They were not part of the street performers hired to lure tourists.

One of them nudged Jimmy in the ribs.

"You looking for early entrance into the club? Maybe some female companionship?"

"...the tugboat...inched away from the mooring."

Ford stared at the tiny man. His sallow skin stood out against the bright red head adornment.

"This is Rutherford Jones from Oakland," he said, pointing at Jimmy.

If the name meant anything to the brightly clad men, they didn't reveal it.

Jimmy took the bold approach.

"We'd like to have a discussion with Warren Lee. Do you boys know how we can find him?"

The two Asians made eye contact but remained neutral.

"We have a message from Wu Chiong of the Nine Blades," Ford ventured.

At the mention of the venerable clan leader, one of the men spat on the sidewalk.

"I see you're not fond of your Oakland brethren," Jimmy observed.

"He is no brethren." The man stated.

Ford could tell these men were just lakeys sent out into the streets as scouts to either detect potential investors or possible threats against the establishment. The huge private eye ventured a direct approach might be less subtle.

"We have knowledge Mr. Lee may find invaluable."

The Chinese man perked up. "Perhaps if you tell me first, I can decide if your information is worth a trip to see Mr. Lee."

Ford grinned and flexed his muscles. "That's all I wanted to hear. Now I know you boys can direct me to him."

"And why would we do that?"

Jimmy couldn't help himself. "I was thinking the same thing."

Ford withdrew his revolver. He dared to bare it in public.

"You would threaten us here, in Chinatown, in broad daylight?" the angry Chinese questioned.

Ford didn't hesitate. He handed the man his gun. This caused Jimmy to release an audible groan.

"A gesture of respect," Ford stated in a monotone voice.

The tiny Asian snatched the gun and deposited it into a side pocket.

"I can not guarantee you will see Mr. Lee, but he will want to hear Wu Chiong's message. We will escort you to him."

Ford bowed in respect. Jimmy repeated the gesture, his bowler spilling from his head.

The quartet paraded down the colorful sidewalks of Chinatown, filled with throngs of shoppers and pedestrians. They arrived at a glitzy office building, surprisingly out of character for the neighborhood, with its American styled deco.

"I was expecting a palace, not an office building," Jimmy noted.

"Be sharp," Ford cautioned.

When they reached the inner office of Warren Lee's modern establishment, Ford and Jimmy were instructed to wait. Much to their relief, they were left alone.

"Why did you give him your gun?" Jimmy demanded.

Ford shrugged. "Didn't think I might need it. Besides, don't even know if the thing works."

Jimmy accepted this explanation. He craved another drink.

"What do you think will happen?"

Ford shrugged again.

"Will you stop shaking your shoulders!" Jimmy barked. "You're not making this easier."

"Sorry, Jimmy."

Just then, the inner door opened and a well-dressed young man entered. He greeted them with a wide smile and a firm handshake. "Welcome, gentlemen, I am Warren Lee."

Ford rose from his chair deliberately, making sure to stretch his body to its full length. Jimmy tried to follow suit, but only stumbled forward to clumsily shake the man's hand.

"I'm Rutherford Jones," Jimmy stated.

The man's smile remained intact. "No, you're not."

Ford offered his handshake, "I'm Jones."

Warren Lee gripped his hand firmly and laughed. "Please forgive my brashness. You don't get to be in my position without being careful. My men over in Oakland are aware of your relationship with my partner Mr. Chiong."

"Partner? That implies equality," Ford quipped.

"Easy Mr. Jones. The Chinese culture has vast differences from your mainstream America. Mr. Chiong may fancy himself as a separate entity, but his vision is narrow."

Jimmy snorted. "The old buzzard could use eye glasses."

Neither Ford nor Lee found this amusing.

"My people respect their elders," Lee admonished. "Wu Chiong comes from a different time. You see I was born here, in the good old US of A. I like to eat hamburgers and I like swing dancing."

"How modern of you," Jimmy sneered.

Warren Lee maintained his friendly manner.

"Forgive my friend, Mr. Lee. We had a very rough night. Some intruders broke into our home and tried to rob us. You can understand why Mr. McGee might be grumpy."

The handsome Asian shook his head in disgust. "Terrible circumstances, my friends. I am happy to report that the vile treachery and hopelessness that has invaded California in recent years has shied away from our little paradise."

"Is that so?" Ford asked.

Enamored of the conversation, the Chinaman continued. "Look around you, my good man. All you see is expansion and growth. Chinatown is the epicenter of San Francisco, and it will even grow more powerful when the white man's dollars begin to flood past our gateway."

"Because of the Bay Bridge?"

"Assuredly, but that's not the only reason. In all modesty, I must claim a huge role in that development."

Jimmy glanced out into the street. "These nightclubs that have popped up in the last year or two. Your idea?"

The Asian grinned even wider if that could be believed.

"My doing," he admitted. "It came at a cost, though. The Chinese elders are not very happy with your government. For over half a century now you have banned immigration from China. In those five decades, those who were here endured and survived. Men like Wu Chiong even prospered."

"But?" Ford bit.

"But I follow a different path. I don't resent the government blockade. In fact, I think it backfired on them. While you true Americans battle hunger and destitution, we Chinese have united and gotten stronger. We take care of our own."

Ford and Jimmy couldn't argue the point.

"Men like Wu Chiong don't want to ruin the establishment. They are content with their tiny place in America, but not me. I want more."

Ford interrupted. "You want to cut out the Oakland gangs?"

Lee's smile vanished abruptly. "Where did that come from? I detest that word gangs. Just as I detest the Nine Blades. It's juvenile. They aim to strong-arm our own hard working people. Chiong has been the guilty party for decades."

"And how do you intend to make a living?" Jimmy ventured.

"Simple, my friend, the American way. Ingenuity and commercialism. I have a plan to bring this economy from out of the stone-age."

"How so?" asked Jimmy.

"By giving the Americans what they want."

"I don't follow."

Lee's smile surfaced again.

"Meat and potatoes."

"Huh?"

"It's the American staple. We just wrap Chinese dressing around it. Let me explain. All these colorful nightclubs offer the finest of Asian cuisine, but unlike old man Chiong and the other dinosaurs, we offer steak. Americans love steak, especially the wealthy folks. Come down to any of our clubs on a weekend and you will see the grill fired up and cattle lining up to be served.

"But it doesn't stop there, oh no. We give you folks what every red blooded man wants."

"What's that?" asked Jimmy.

Ford answered before Lee could.

"He means girls Jimmy."

Lee snapped his fingers. "Right. Again, we dress it up in Asian wrapping paper. Chinese chorus girls take the stage wearing the traditional modest *cheongsams*. The crowd eats it up. Men convince themselves that they are witnessing a classy, elegant show. But that's not what you desire, is it, Mr. McGee?"

Jimmy shrugged. "I'd rather go down to the ports and catch a glimpse of flesh."

Lee chuckled. "Correct again, my friend. That is why underneath the traditional robe, the chorus girls wear bathing suits. It's all just a distraction to make men part with their money."

"But Wu Chiong and the elders don't care for your new ways of earning," Ford guessed.

Warren Lee sighed. "Wu Chiong is a respected man, but only among Asians. He distrusts the white man and thus shuts out potential avenues of revenue. If my people are to grow strong and prosperous, old ways like this must be shunted."

"Permanently?" Jimmy wondered.

A grimace drifted over the young man's face. "That is entirely up to Wu Chiong."

Ford rubbed at his chin. "Did you cut off his messenger's hand?"

The starkness of the question rattled Warren Lee. "Were you not listening to anything I said, gentlemen? Did I infer any illegal activities in my explanation of my financial plans?"

Ford and Jimmy didn't reply.

Warren Lee withdrew a revolver and pointed it at them.

"What gives?" demanded Jimmy.

The Chinaman smiled. "Just a demonstration. You see my reaction represented the old way, Chiong's way."

"And your way?" Ford asked.

Lee handed him the gun. Ford was startled to recognize it as his own.

"I believe you left this with one of my scouts, a respectable gesture. I return it to you in good faith and leave you with this thought. Mr. Chiong's ways are antiquated and can only speed up the decline of Western civilization. There are countries that see us as weak. They will soon grow bold and aggressive unless we change our ways. I offer an alternative, not just for Asians, but all Americans. Once again, I remind you, I was born here, and as such this is my country. I obey all laws, Mr. Jones."

"And the severed hand?"

"Not my work. Too messy. I'm of the new school of thought that a legal solution to problems is the way of the future."

Warren Lee held open the outer door for the pair.

"Thank you for seeing us, Mr. Lee."

"Do not be a stranger Mr. Jones. I understand you have a relationship with a certain unemployed singer?"

Ford grew tense at the mention of Myra.

"Relax, my friend. I just wanted to inform you of the progress my people have made. I understand she can not even sing on the same stage as some of her musical band members? Not to mention, traveling in certain hotels is forbidden?"

Ford nodded sadly.

"We Chinese do not discriminate in that way. All our performers are treated equally. Think of this when you return to Oakland. Let your mind roll with the idea of what that city could be like if men such as Wu Chiong were to be replaced."

Ford didn't answer. He simply vacated the premises. Jimmy lingered a bit longer.

"You have something to add Mr. McGee?"

The skinny youth swallowed hard. "If I'm to believe you weren't behind the attack on Chiong's fella, then who was?"

Lee remained stoic. He simply waved Jimmy through the doorway.

"Look within, Mr. McGee. A snake usually hides among its prey."

• • •

The journey back to Oakland was uneventful. Ford actually enjoyed the leisurely pace of the rumbling ferry boat. He dined on a pair of hot dogs while Jimmy McGee caught a few winks on deck. The apprehension they had felt earlier in the day regarding Warren Lee had vanished.

Ford felt the young businessman was genuine. His influence had spread beyond the secretive walls of Chinatown to mainstream society. Warren Lee was a mover and shaker. That fact was undeniable. The real question regarded his intentions toward the elder Chinese clans. Was he sincere in shifting to legitimate revenue or was that all a façade Ford and Jimmy had encountered? It was still too early to tell.

And then there was the severed hand.

Wu Chiong had expressed genuine fear, a side of the iron ruler that Ford had never witnessed before. Perhaps Warren Lee had indeed adapted some of the ancient ways.

Jimmy stirred restlessly. The frail youth hadn't eaten since the early morning, and his complexion was deathly pale. Ford wondered if the poor youth had damaged his vital organs binging on rotgut consumption.

"One more drink…" Jimmy mumbled.

Ford shook him roughly.

"Wake up Jimmy. We're pulling into port. I want to start moving to the head of the boat so we can beat the traffic back to our office."

Jimmy wiped spittle from his chin and listened to his stomach churning.

"Once I get chow in me, I'll be good to go."

"Go where?" Ford asked.

"To see Wu Chiong, of course," Jimmy replied.

Ford pondered the idea. "There's not much to tell him. We can't be sure Warren Lee killed that messenger."

"Maybe not, but somebody did. And that somebody must have a brass pair to think they can pull that act on old man Chiong. I hear he once pulled off all the fingernails on a cook who took home a few bags of rice."

Ford nodded in solemn agreement. He too had heard the tales of Wu Chiong's savagery. The Oakland underworld had many factions, mobsters from all over the world, but one thing they had in common was a respect for the Chinese. No one dared to extort a thin dime from wizened warlord Wu Chiong.

"I don't think Lee is trying to muscle in on Oakland. It just doesn't make sense right now. His empire is expanding like crazy. The locals told me all his clubs are booked to the hilt for the grand opening of the Bay Bridge. "

Jimmy agreed. "Yeah, I heard MGM tried to get him to cater a private party for the glam crowd, but Lee couldn't accommodate the crowd. He has more business than he can handle right now."

"That's why I doubt he'd try to snuff out the Nine Blades right now."

The pair remained silent the remainder of the voyage and managed to maneuver to the front when the boat docked at the mooring. They bypassed the circus-like atmosphere on the pier while making their way to the side street they had parked the car on.

"Son of a gun! Do you see what I see?" Jimmy asked, whistling softly.

Ford did indeed see what his partner was gawking at. Toward the front of the pier was the colorful chubby man who had conned them out of their money. The rotund man was in deep concentration working his charms on a young couple.

"I'm going to smack him right on both his chins!" Jimmy claimed.

Ford only smiled. He had a better plan. They raced up the pier, careful not to let the huckster see them coming. It took all Jimmy's restraint not to heave the man into the chilly depths of the murky water.

"Ahoy, friend!" Ford called out in his most jovial manner.

Distracted, the chunky man turned to see who was seeking his attention. His smile froze when he saw the familiar pair.

"Good day, gentlemen. I hope we are not going to have a problem over our earlier misunderstanding?" He raised both hand in the air as if surrendering.

Ford kept up the pretense of being joyful. The young couple seemed confused. The man, a well-dressed, vacation-type sort, had a dollar bill in his hand. It was obvious he intended to impress his date by leaving a generous tip for the brightly clad salesman.

"Can we get the tickets now?" the man's date asked. She was a healthy young blonde, her good looks sparing her from the life of poverty most Californians endured.

The chubby man coughed nervously. He flinched when Jimmy took a step forward.

"Don't let us interrupt," he said. "These fine young folks want to get on their way."

The young man relaxed; satisfied that Jimmy was no threat.

"Thank you, sir. Did you take up our friend here on his generous offer?" He cocked a thumb in the huckster's direction.

"We surely did." Ford chimed in, flashing an exaggerated smile. The huge man chuckled, his girth heaving up and down. A sheen of perspiration dotted his forehead despite the November chill.

"Ahem, thank you for the kind recommendation, gents. Now if you'll just give me a moment with this fine young couple…"

"It's our anniversary," the blonde piped in. "I mean, we're not married or anything, not yet."

Her date blushed, nervous at the attention.

"It's been three beautiful months, hasn't it my sweet?"

The girl hugged his arm tightly. "We're taking a ride over to San Francisco to meet my parents."

Jimmy shook the young man's hand. "That's a big step on the road to matrimony."

"Yes, yes it is." The chubby man said, wiping away the excess moisture.

Ford couldn't resist. "Good thing they stopped here. Isn't it?"

The con man nodded. He had no idea how this would play out, but one look at Ford's huge biceps made him wobble.

"That's right," said Jimmy, catching Ford's drift. "Wharf Charters runs a weekly promotion rewarding one lucky couple and something tells me you fine folks are going to walk away with that prize."

"We are?" gushed the girl.

Ford made eye contact with the salesman. The blob was starting to quiver. He knew he was in a situation he couldn't extract himself from. Sucking in a mouthful of sea air, he summoned up his most dramatic voice.

"Of course, you are!"

The young couple hugged wildly, excitement coursing through them. Even Jimmy felt a tinge of electricity in the air. He hung on the showman's words.

"You two kids get to enjoy the romantic slow ride of the ferry this evening courtesy of Wharf Charters." He banged on his wooden sign.

The couple began to jump up and down but then stopped in their tracks.

"The ferry? But you said it would take forever, and I want to get there before my parents are asleep," the girl protested.

Ford intervened. "Oh, but that was before he knew about your anniversary."

"That's correct," the nervous hawker spat.

Jimmy seized the opportunity.

"He was just setting you up for the real reward!"

The beautiful blonde perked right back up. "He was?"

"Indeed," Ford sang. "You lovebirds are going to take that long slow ride. Sure you'll be delayed but your parents will understand once you tell them what happened."

The boyfriend stared at Ford, marveling at his muscular frame.

"Tell me about it, friend."

Ford bowed and pointed at the sweaty con man. "Don't mess this up."

The heavy set man saw the determination in Ford's eyes. He knew the big man was serious.

"He's right friends. Anniversaries are special and this one will be spectacular."

The blonde swooned at the words dripping off the fat man's tongue. It inspired him to raise the level of his performance.

"Not only do we pay for your ferry ride, but I personally am throwing in some extra cash so you fine folks can have a romantic dinner as you watch the waves roll by."

Jimmy nudged the young man. "He ain't done yet."

"I'm not?" the big man whispered. "I mean, I'm not! Just to get you started on the road to a long and prosperous life together, my company is gifting you wonderful young lovers a whopping five dollars to enjoy on the other side of the bay."

Ford was satisfied. Jimmy wasn't.

"Tell them about the bonus prize."

The fat man almost choked.

"You did remember the bonus prize?" Jimmy continued.

The perky blonde began to tremble. "My goodness, pinch me! This can't be happening."

"I wish someone would pinch me," the fat man mumbled.

"What was that?" Ford begged.

"I was just getting to the bonus," the big man exhaled. He rubbed a grimy hand over his pencil thin mustache. "I almost forgot to add that you folks are going to get an extra five dollars so you can repeat the experience on your way back!"

The blonde couldn't contain herself. She leapt at the fat man and pecked her dreamy lips on his cheek.

"It's fate! Fate, I tell you. I knew this would be the best day of my life."

She hugged the man around his neck until he had to push her away. He handed her date a ten dollar bill reluctantly.

"Enjoy your night," he offered in a monotone voice.

The couple shook hands with Ford and Jimmy before departing down the pier. The girl came running back on high heels, her shapely calves flashing skin from beneath her form fitting dress.

She hugged the huge man one more time.

"For good luck," she stated, hustling back to her waiting boyfriend.

Ford and Jimmy waited for the couple to get out of earshot before accosting the garish figure.

"That was some stunt you pulled on us!" Jimmy growled.

The fat man snorted. "Look who is talking! You boys just swindled me out of two days pay!"

Ford's eyes grew preposterously wide.

"Say what? You make five dollars a day working this con?"

The chunky man grew nervous.

"That does it!" Jimmy snarled. Before Ford could restrain him, the huffy Irishman pushed the blobby man off the boardwalk and splashing into the murky water.

Ford was stunned.

"Are you crazy?"

Jimmy giggled like a child. "Look at him!" he pointed at the huckster who was bobbing up and down, gasping for air.

The man shook an angry fist at Jimmy.

A handful of gawkers started to gather, many unaware of the events that led up to the man's unplanned swim.

"That poor man!"

"He may drown!"

"Someone call the authorities. I think that black man may have shoved him!"

Ford and Jimmy didn't need to be prompted. They sprung into action, hurtling down the boardwalk and away from the commotion. It wasn't until they reached the safety of their automobile that they slowed down.

Jimmy was winded; his usually pale face now a scarlet red.

Ford felt invigorated by the run, his body weary after the long boat ride. He slapped Jimmy on the back, harder than necessary.

"What's the big deal?" the skinny youth demanded.

Ford revved up the engine on the sedan.

"You did okay, Mister McGee."

Jimmy grinned. "Well, at least those young kids will enjoy a starry night."

Ford sobered up. "Let's get home and check on our own ladies, pal."

•   •   •

Rutherford Jones was relieved to find his girlfriend, Myra, waiting for him when he got home. She stood outside the apartment stoop, splendidly draped in a bright canary yellow dress, totally out of season, but still wearable in sunny Oakland.

She greeted him warmly with a hug and a sensual kiss.

"Everything OK?" he inquired.

She flashed a set of perfectly white teeth.

"It is now handsome."

Linda Mae sprung out of the doorway a moment later, her hands dabbing at her freshly made up hair. She had taken the extra time to smear on lipstick for Jimmy.

"You're back!" she declared.

Jimmy McGee grinned and bowed.

"You would think we traveled to Arabia! What gives with the homecoming?"

Linda Mae leaped the final stair to land in his arms. She nearly bowled him over.

"Oh Jimmy, something's in the air. We keep seeing patrol cars speed by."

"Did they have the sirens blaring?" Ford asked.

Linda Mae shook her head. "No, just a constant stream of policemen up and down the avenue."

"It looked like a blue parade!" Myra added.

Ford tried to quell their anxiety.

"It's just them getting ready for the opening of the Bay Bridge. It's a pretty big deal. I hear the President, himself, wants to make a trip down to see it."

"Ah, just a bunch of boring steel girders if you ask me," Jimmy blathered.

"It may have saved our economy, Jimmy. The millions of dollars spent on that bridge have eased up the depression around these parts. People are employed now."

"She's right, you know," Linda Mae chimed in. "I've been pouring over my books and sales are up. Granted, we're talking pennies, but it's an improvement."

Bottles McGee remained pessimistic. "Just the fat cats slumming in these parts for cheap jewelry, baby. The little folks are still fighting over bread crumbs."

Myra changed the subject.

"Did you boys resolve the issue with those dimwitted burglars?"

Ford didn't want to discuss specifics of the case. He stared at her curvy body in the sundress.

"Aren't you cold?"

Myra frowned. "I'm wearing this for you."

"I like it," Jimmy mumbled, prompting Linda Mae to elbow him.

"Listen, girls, let's make plans for tonight. Jimmy and I have to travel into Chinatown to see a client, so maybe we can get that out of the way and be back in time to treat you ladies to a prime rib dinner."

Linda Mae shook her head at Ford.

"Always meat with you fellas. No wonder, you resemble a tree trunk. How about we try that new place in town. I hear they serve exquisite French food."

Jimmy cleared his throat loudly.

"Are you forgetting something?" he asked, his eyes darting back and forth between Ford and Myra.

Linda Mae was clueless.

"You don't like French food either?" she asked her roommate.

Myra didn't respond.

Ford answered in a polite tone.

"She does enjoy French food, Linda Mae."

"Well, what is the problem, Rufus?"

Jimmy grabbed his girlfriend by the arm and swung her toward him.

"Linda Mae, baby, you know about that French place?"

The ditzy blonde made an over the top gesture of gyrating her arms above her head.

"Of course I know. I read the reviews in the Daily. The chef is marvelous, why I heard…"

Jimmy placed a finger at her lips to hush her.

"They don't serve black folks."

Linda Mae was too caught up in her wonderment to listen. She continued to babble on. "I heard the wait can be so long on a weekend, but we…"

"Did you hear what I said?" Jimmy interrupted.

The older woman grew quiet.

"Good," Jimmy answered. "Go in the house and get ready. Ford and I will need a few minutes in the office and then we can head out."

Linda Mae remained silent, her face an image of puzzlement.

"Is there a problem?" Jimmy asked, not rudely.

She remained stoic, but shook her head slightly. After awhile, she turned and marched back into her storefront. Jimmy waited until she had disappeared from sight, before turning toward Ford and Myra. The pair stood silent, waiting for him to speak. Jimmy forced himself to give them a polite smile before he turned and headed in after his woman.

Ford hugged Myra.

"It will be okay," she whispered.

"I know."

•   •   •

Oakland's little Chinatown paled in comparison to what Ford and Jimmy had enjoyed in San Francisco. There were none of the spectacular nightclubs or tourist gardens that greeted visitors on the other side of the Bay. In stark contrast, the tight-knit neighborhood survived on a commerce populated by take-out restaurants, over-sized laundry-mats and small brick mortar stores catering to customers clutching on to the ancient ways with watered down versions of medicines and herbs being passed off as authentic.

It was a steady stream of revenue, all tightly controlled under the watchful eye of Wu Chiong and his Nine Blades clan. The elderly leader was notorious for visiting shop owners himself, threatening mayhem and destruction if his weekly shakedowns weren't adhered to.

Lately, Chiong had eased up on his daily regimen, handing off more chores to his second in command, Denny. The younger Chinaman had impressed his leader by building up a sizable side business down at the wharf. Denny had managed to create a side empire, headlined with bare knuckle brawls and illegal smuggling. His reputation had grown immensely under the tutelage of the elder Chiong.

As such, he had grown weary of the old man's fondness for Ford and Jimmy. Denny despised the alcoholic Irishman and he didn't trust any black Americans. One thing he did agree with old man Chiong was keeping the trust within their own kind.

Dressed immaculately in a new black suit and shiny loafers, Denny greeted the two investigators and their dates stiffly as they entered Chiong's restaurant.

"Back to dine at our establishment again?" he asked as the quartet entered the rickety corner shop.

Jimmy strolled out front and center.

"Ladies, this is Denny, a friend of ours."

The young Chinaman forced himself to be polite.

"Mr. McGee and Mr. Jones, a pleasure to see you with female companionship. My mother was correct."

"About what?" Jimmy asked suspiciously.

"That there is hope for all."

Ford pointed to the two armed men on the winding staircase.

"I trust our dates will be safe at the bar?"

Denny smiled, his eyes ogling Myra after a brief glance at Linda Mae.

"Rest assured, I will see to it personally."

This angered Ford even more so as Myra smiled appreciatively at the young Asian.

"This place is beautiful. Why haven't you taken us here before?" the question was aimed at Ford, but her eyes never left Denny.

The young man grinned widely.

"You grace us with your beauty, miss?"

She smiled coyly.

"Myra…Myra Ellington."

"And I'm Linda Mae," her blonde friend intervened. 'Do you have any of those fancy drinks that come with a miniature umbrella? I always wanted to see what those looked like."

Denny extended an arm for both women.

"If you will accompany me, I'd be happy to give you a tour of our humble restaurant."

Ford tapped his foot impatiently.

"Is your employer expecting us?"

Denny forced himself to avert his gaze from Myra Ellington's alluring cleavage long enough to address the two men.

"Please, do take your time."

Jimmy McGee shook his head in wonderment.

"Don't get too comfortable, Denny. We plan on dining at a restaurant that doesn't get its meat from the back alley."

Denny laughed from deep in his belly and gave Jimmy a slap on the back, making sure his palm struck the frail youth's spine hard enough to jar him.

"Such a prankster, Mr. McGee!"

Jimmy stumbled forward, wanting to turn and sucker punch the man, but he caught himself as he spotted Linda Mae soaking in the atmosphere. He remembered that she hadn't really gotten out much before or since she had met him. Squashing his anger, he allowed a smile to grace his lips.

"Make sure she gets one of those umbrellas, friend."

Linda Mae giggled like a school girl as she departed with Denny and

Myra. Several of the diners spun in their chairs to watch Myra shimmy toward the bar. Resigned to the fact that the girls were enamored of the place, Ford and Jimmy headed up the flight of stairs.

Jimmy lifted his arms for the pat-down.

The bodyguard shook his head.

"Not tonight. You would not be foolish enough to entertain any evil thought while your companions are with Denny."

"Makes sense." The young Irishman muttered, letting himself in the doorway with Ford following suit.

Wu Chiong looked older than usual, which is hard to believe since he already resembled a corpse. He rose awkwardly from his chair and greeted them. Ford couldn't help but notice he was barefoot.

"I wish to hear your news."

Ford shrugged, "Not much to tell. We met Warren Lee. He denied cutting off your messenger's hand."

"And you believe him?"

"We do."

Wu Chiong settled back in his chair, his body shrunken inside a dark purple robe. He remained silent for a long time.

"Don't tell me he fell asleep? Or worse?" Jimmy wondered out loud.

Ford was about to jostle the old man when the Chinaman's eyes bulged out.

"Warren Lee is a liar."

The words came out slow and deliberately. They were expressionless, but Ford and Jimmy didn't need to inquire about the old man's feelings.

"He has a good thing going," Jimmy explained. "The money is pouring in. Not just local money either. That kid has reeled in the big fish from Hollywood and California heights."

Ford agreed. "Plus this Bay Bridge opening in a couple of days will make him the most powerful man in San Francisco. Those trendy nightclubs are a means to make money."

The old man didn't comment. He simply asked, "You don't think he was behind the attack?"

Jimmy snorted. "Look wrinkles, you're a straight shooter, so I'll lay it out for you. You're no threat to the man. The Nine Blades are a dying notion. This is America, we have laws. You can't keep strong-arming folks for money. Warren Lee saw that. He focused his efforts on legal income, and it worked. I say hats off to the man."

Wu Chiong nodded and his eyes drifted to Ford, compelling him to chime in.

"If you'll accompany me…"

"Jimmy is correct about Warren Lee."

Chiong allowed the comments to soak in. He rose without assistance and held his door open for the two men.

"Thank you for the report."

"About the money…" Ford began.

The decrepit man waved him off, "A deal is a deal."

Ford shook his hand and departed. Jimmy lingered a moment.

"You look like you want to say something to me, pruneface?"

Chiong snarled and flashed his yellow teeth.

"You are wrong about the Nine Blades dying."

Jimmy didn't want to hedge his luck.

"Be careful Chiong. You've built yourself a nice little empire here. Be a shame to toss it away over jealously. You were once a young buck like Warren Lee. Let him have his cake."

"Interesting suggestion."

•　•　•

The joyous couples spent a robust evening at the Black Falcon on the waterfront. It was a cut above the usual weeknight fare hosted by Oakland's entertainment scene. A decent crowd of about thirty had ventured out to witness a baby-faced crooner spitting out popular tunes with a warbly voice.

Myra wasn't impressed by the act, but she was happy as punch that Ford had taken them along. She still couldn't understand his hostility toward Denny. She knew Ford not to be the jealous type, but his dislike of the young Chinaman was all too evident.

"You know I was just being polite with Denny." She offered as they danced during one of the slow songs.

Ford shrugged. "Not a problem, baby."

"So why did you keep giving him daggers?"

"I just pick up the wrong vibe from that guy. He's a very shady character. At least with old man Chiong, you know where you stand. Denny, he's another cat altogether."

Myra nodded in the direction of Jimmy and Linda Mae. There were several empty bottles lined up in front of them.

"It's amazing that they never put on an ounce of weight!"

Ford studied his partner intently. Jimmy McGee was twenty-five years old, Linda Mae, a full ten years older. The pair represented an accurate picture of west coast America. People were getting by. The struggle was evident on their outward appearances, but the veil of hope mirrored on their faces foreshadowed the future. Ford wondered if it would be the same for black folks.

"That little scene about the French restaurant tonight, did you get a sense Linda Mae was holding back?"

Myra shook her head. "It's only natural. Look at her upbringing. She never interacted outside her own race before and now she's thrust into living amongst us. With the economy so bad we even become a competition to her."

"Yes, but does she regret us being in her life?"

"Oh, no, Ford. That girl and I have our differences, but I can tell a good soul when I encounter one. She's good people. I think she was more angry with society than not being able to attend some snobby restaurant."

Ford gave it some thought. "You're right. Sometimes, I forget that other folks face discrimination as well. I didn't think too much of it before, but that woman has overcome a lot. She's a business owner in a man's world. And she's making the best of it. I wonder if it's time to stop playing this charade with her."

The beautiful singer raised an eyebrow.

Ford continued. "She has to know that my name is not Rufus. I mean, you slip up almost every day and Jimmy. Well, he gets a loose tongue when the booze starts working."

Myra stopped him.

"Ford, I think Linda Mae is aware that you're the boss, not Jimmy."

A look of incredulity escaped Ford.

"You do?"

"Yes."

"So why does she act like I'm just a big lug hired to restock the firewood?"

Myra sighed. "Same reason everyone else does. It's easier that way."

"How so?"

A melancholy look formed on her lovely face. "Because they're scared. People are afraid of change, Rutherford. Linda Mae is no different than all these other folks in here."

She waved an arm at the other patrons of the Black Falcon.

"These people have been faced with so much lately. Lack of money, dreams dashed, and now we're asking them to accept us as equals. It just happened too fast."

"Warren Lee made a comment about how the Chinese didn't

discriminate. He was mocking us Americans. Sad thing is, I think he was right."

Myra glanced over at their friends. Jimmy had shed his bow tie, and Linda Mae's hair had fallen about her shoulders. They looked relaxed, maybe even relieved.

The drunk couple caught her stare, and waved at her. Jimmy raised his beer in a toast as he guzzled the remainder.

Myra smiled accordingly and hugged Ford even tighter.

The baby-faced crooner finished his number and thanked the crowd. He appeared to still be in his teens, a hint of acne dotting his face. Myra and Ford strolled casually to the table and sat down.

Linda Mae hiccupped once.

"Beg your pardon." She croaked, a tinge of red highlighting her complexion. "Rufus, you are the biggest man on the dance floor. I must say you tower over the other gentlemen."

Ford smiled politely. "Actually, Linda Mae my name…"

Jimmy caught a waitress passing by. "Sweetie, keep em coming over here!"

Myra declined hers. She sat uncomfortably across from her companions.

"You should be up there doll. Your voice is like honey."

"He's right, young lady." Linda Mae echoed. "That youngster they have up there should still be in diapers. And, I can't be sure, but I think he's messing up the words."

Myra forced herself to smile. She wanted so badly to explain that the boy's singing was fine. It was just that Linda Mae was drunk.

"Maybe we should order some more food?" Ford offered. He was hoping the nourishment would help soak up the alcohol.

Jimmy rubbed his belly. "Nah, I'm good. Couldn't eat another bite."

Linda Mae threw in her two cents. "We just dined an hour ago."

Ford stared at the dozen bottles in front of him. They had consumed the load in the short time they had been there.

"I was about to tell you something, Linda Mae."

The ditzy blonde opened her eyes wide. "Don't spoil it Rufus!"

Ford shot her a look of confusion.

"Let Jimmy make his announcement."

"Announcement?" Myra begged.

Jimmy McGee rapped a spoon against one of the empty beer bottles. He rose on two unsteady legs, knocking over a half filled vase that adorned the table.

The dirty water rolled toward Ford who quietly stopped the flow with the edge of the table cloth. Jimmy was oblivious to his actions.

"I want to make a toast," the drunken Irishman warbled.

"To good friends." Ford blurted out.

Jimmy nodded, tipping his glass. He was surprised to find it empty. "Someone stole my drink!"

Linda Mae howled in delight. "My Jimmy, such a kidder! Don't you just love him?"

Myra groaned. She noticed the splotches of beer on Linda Mae's dress. It was one of the new one's she had purchased at Carvers. The stain would be permanent.

"Listen, honey. I have to use the little girl's room. Can you come with me? You know I get nervous going alone."

Linda Mae grew bold. "Absolutely, darling. It will give James time to compose his words."

Jimmy barked. "Compose? Like, make a song or something? Maybe I could recite a few dirty limericks, but mama McGee didn't raise no composer."

"Go ahead, ladies," Ford commanded.

Myra grabbed Linda Mae's hand, careful to make sure her friend was steady. Much to her surprise, Linda Mae's reflexes were fine. She was a much better drinker than Jimmy.

"We will be a moment," she said grabbing up her napkin in hopes of washing the beer stains from her roommates dress.

Jimmy sat back down as the two girls departed. He reached again for his empty glass.

"Stop it, Jimmy!" Ford growled, "You're overdoing it!"

The Irishman was defiant. "You would deny a man a drink on this important day?"

"What are you gabbing about?"

He belched loudly. "Rutherford, my good man, I'm going to ask Linda Mae to marry me!"

Ford fluttered his lips. "Oh, brother!"

Jimmy rose again. "Where is that waitress?"

The young girl glanced over. Ford caught her eyes and shook his head no. The girl nodded discreetly and disappeared back to the kitchen area.

"Hey!" yelled Jimmy.

When the girl didn't return, he sat down frustrated. "I'm not leaving that lass a tip!"

"Jimmy, I appreciate your intentions, and nothing would make me happier than seeing you and Linda Mae tie the knot, but don't ruin it like this!"

The Irishman rubbed at his nose. "Ruin it? How?"

Ford didn't want to hurt his friend's feelings.

"Answer me, damn it!"

Ford placed a firm hand on Jimmy's arm.

"Tone it down, Jimmy." He relaxed his grip when the anger faded from his partner's face. "For one thing, the moment ain't right."

Jimmy spun his head around. "What's wrong with it? This place is fancy enough, and I'm wearing my Sunday best."

Ford conjured up a quick response.

"You ain't got no ring!"

A defeated look surfaced on Jimmy. "Well, damn, Ford, I hadn't thought about it. Linda Mae is surrounded by rings all day. I figured another one wouldn't make a difference."

Ford carried the ball.

"Nonsense! All women want a ring, a diamond ring!"

"Diamonds!"

Ford rose to his full height. "Damn skippy! And no fake glass ones like Linda Mae deals in. Nope, you've got to get her a real one. A nice big shiny one!"

Distracted, Jimmy forgot about his beer.

"From a reputable place?"

Ford nodded. "Of course! Remember, this is a one time deal. If you get her a speck of dust, people will notice and they'll remember."

"For real?"

"Amen!"

Jimmy slumped back into his chair, deep in concentration. The nervousness of the situation had caused him to start to sober up. He snapped his fingers hard.

"Coffee! I need coffee!"

The waitress heard him. She scurried over with a fresh pot. She had been ready to call the doormen if Jimmy had got out of control.

"Keep it coming, doll!" Jimmy ordered.

Ford chuckled as his friend gulped at the steaming java.

"The roof of your mouth will be sore tomorrow!" he warned.

Jimmy ignored him, slurping at his caffeine.

"Man oh man! You saved me again Ford. I would never have lived it down if I proposed tonight! You're a good friend."

Ford nodded calmly, the anxiety fading. "You too, Jimmy."

• • •

An hour later and four cups of coffee later for Jimmy McGee, the quartet had retreated to the comfort of a local diner, Alma's, for one last hurrah before calling it a night.

The local diner was filled with truck drivers, eager to refill their sleep deprived bodies with a jolt of caffeine for the final hours before dawn.

The roadside diner was bustling with activity, most of it chatty but efficient. Ford was happy to frequent Almas. The coffee was always fresh and the stares were never unfriendly.

He poured a generous helping of sugar into his cup while waiting for a slice of apple pie to cool off. The others had declined food, claiming the hour was late. Fortunately, the diner didn't serve alcohol so Jimmy and Linda Mae were finally drifting back to earth.

Ford stared at the plate glass windows. There were a couple of drunk revelers swaying down the sidewalks, but no other foot traffic. The streets were eerily silent. He felt himself beginning to nod off a couple of times.

Myra Ellington still looked good for the late hour. Ford honestly couldn't recall a time she didn't look splendid. The woman was naturally beautiful. He caught himself smiling at her boyishly.

The curvy siren returned his coy smile. She had enjoyed their double date. The drinking aside, Jimmy and Linda Mae always provided soothing conversation and she could truly say she enjoyed their company. Ford, himself, always behaved better when they were together as a group.

Linda Mae showed the effect of the booze wearing off. She frequently rubbed at her temples and, for the most part, was breathing through her mouth rather than her nostrils. She looked as if she had slept in the glittery silver gown she wore. The beer stains not apparent unless one really inspected it up close. She had somehow lost her hairpin, but she wasn't too worried about that. The jewelry shop was filled with replacements that probably would never sell.

Jimmy McGee sat stoically in his chair, contemplating his intended deeds that had fallen through. He had a pattern of drinking and getting boisterous. He liked to blame it on his Irish heritage, but he knew the guilt lay within. He was addicted to alcohol, unable to go a full day without touching a drop. It had led to various encounters in his life, most of which had ended regretfully. Ford was the exception. Jimmy had been frequenting a local pub back in the day when Ford had been denied admission. Jimmy had piped up that everyone deserved to enjoy a hard drink, especially the poison being doled out in this particular establishment. The owner hadn't taken too kindly to the jab. He had ordered two burly bouncers to deposit Jimmy's hide into the back alley.

When Jimmy had resisted departure, the two men had made it a point to make the bony Irishman an example to other rowdy patrons. They had begun to administer a pounding to his tiny frame. Unable to put up a decent defense, Jimmy was quickly succumbing to a brutal thrashing.

Things may have even turned fatal had Rutherford Jones not decided to stick around that evening. Ford was bored, and since no other tavern would admit him, he had decided to get some fresh air into his lungs. Upon seeing the oversized goons engage the dwarfish Jimmy in fisticuffs, Ford had reacted immediately.

He took his time delivering punishment to the overzealous bouncers. One man would undoubtedly be taking his meals through a straw for months. The other probably would be exempt from any future military drafts, his limbs permanently damaged.

The skinny Irish lad had been grateful ever since. He never questioned Ford's race, nor background. He had immediately invited him back to his apartment to sleep it off and enjoy a bottle of homegrown rotgut. The two men had remained friends ever since.

There was no question Ford would be asked to serve as best man at the wedding. Jimmy didn't care that his burly partner was neither white nor catholic, it didn't matter. He was a friend, a best friend, who had become more of a brother than any of the huge McGee clan.

Jimmy smothered another freshly brewed cup of Alma's house blend.

The man must have a bottomless bladder, Ford wondered, never having seen Jimmy make a pit stop. The big man's day-dreaming was blunted by the noisy roar of fire alarms coming to life.

All of the patrons of Almas rose simultaneously to race toward the plate glass windows. They fought for a view as Engine Company number One rushed by the deserted street, intent on breaking speed records to get to their destination.

A rumble of questions bounced through the crowd. Ford quickly determined the location of the fire was close by. His ears perked up when he heard one of the truck drivers mention Chinatown.

Ford grabbed the waitress and handed her some money. It was more than the bill, but he didn't wait for his change. Instead, he raced for the exit, pulling on his jacket as he ran.

Jimmy McGee gulped a final mouthful of coffee before ordering the two women to remain behind. He knew it wouldn't do any good. Both Myra and Linda Mae were modern headstrong women, neither afraid to get their hands dirty.

It was just that Jimmy knew they couldn't keep up, not in their high heels and slitted gowns. Vainly, he raced after Ford.

It was like a turtle chasing a greyhound. The dark skinned man was almost around the bend before Jimmy had made his way through the doorway. The skinny Irishman caught a glimpse of Ford's jacket as he vanished from sight.

A throng of thrill seekers had followed the sounds of the siren, all intent on making their way to the scene of the fire. Jimmy fought his way through the crowd, no longer dependent on the blare of the sirens. His nostrils caught wind of the burning timber in the air.

Renewing his effort Jimmy plundered forward toward the raging inferno.

Meanwhile, Ford had used his athletic prowess to outdistance the surging mob. His blazing speed had allowed him to reach the scene only moments after the fire truck.

He felt his heart sink as he realized where he was.

Chinatown!

The inferno had engulfed the entrance to Wu Chiong's Laundromat. The building was unsalvageable. Ford only prayed no had been sleeping inside. The deadly flames began to chew at the adjacent restaurant, the same one Ford and his friends had departed earlier in the evening.

Ford saw a handful of firefighters at the huge wooden doorway. They were in a tight-knit circle all pulling and tugging on metal.

The huge man's mouth went agape as he saw the object of their frustration. A heavy metal chain had been used to wrap up the door handles that opened the archway to the restaurant. The firemen fought valiantly to untangle it as the embers began to grow.

Desperately, Ford spun around. He saw several firefighters unraveling a huge fire hose in an effort to end the fiery destruction. He saw that his help wasn't needed there. He continued to watch as the men labored at their efforts to open the bolted doorway.

Ford raced toward the side of the fire truck. He had spotted a glint of metal in the fiery orange glow that was engulfing the street. His eyes detected a long, sturdy fire ax, attached to the side of the truck.

Immediately, he extracted it.

Heaving the long handled ax like a baseball bat, he raced toward the doorway. The firemen parted from it, fearful that he was a madman driven by fear. Ford was grateful for their fright. It allowed him a clean avenue to attack the chain.

Lifting the mighty ax over his head, he chopped down with all his strength. The links buckled and the chain snapped. Ford retreated as firemen tugged at the doorway. As the wooden doors opened a gush of thick black smoke followed. It choked everyone within footsteps.

The fire chief ordered everyone to step back. He waved the other firefights over. They had untangled the thick hoses and had turned on the powerful water flow.

A stream of rushing water exited the hose as three men held it firmly. The result was even more black smoke as the flames were smothered at the entrance.

Ford's eyes drifted upward to the second-floor offices. He could see shadows darting back and forth frantically from above.

People were trapped inside the blazing inferno!

The firefighters were battling the first floor competently but the deadly blaze had already ascended to the top floor. There was no hope to get inside and extinguish the hot flames.

Jimmy McGee came racing toward the scene, his pale skin glowing oddly in the colorful glare of the inferno. He made eye contact with Ford without saying a word. Ford knew the youth was sober enough to be safe. He turned his attention back to the occupants of the second floor.

Fortunately, they hadn't shattered the windows, which would only allow oxygen to feed the ravenous blaze. Instead, the shadows had continued to race back and forth. This would prove fruitless, as it would only serve to utilize the precious air in their lungs.

By this time, frightened residents in the Chinatown neighborhood had awakened. They were scared but determined to battle the deadly fire. They began to form an assembly line of people, passing buckets of water toward the front of Chiong's shop.

Rutherford Jones saw the hopelessness of the situation. The first floor was under siege. Any means of reaching the staircase would prove useless. The choking smoke wouldn't allow for entrance. The firefighters only hoped to stop the spread to neighboring buildings. Chiong's establishment was beyond salvation.

A wrinkled Chinese woman tugged at Ford's jacket as she handed him a half-filled bucket of water. The woman barked at him in Chinese, and then in frustration pushed him toward the fire.

Ford held his ground as he studied the scene. An idea came to him.

He turned the bucket on himself and poured its contents on his head. He raced back and forth grabbing buckets from the residents and dousing himself with water. The angry Chinese screamed and hurled insults, not sure why the dark man was hindering the battle.

Once Ford felt he was sufficiently soaked, he tore off his jacket and wrapped it around his hands. He waved frantically for Jimmy McGee to approach him.

Jimmy couldn't hear a word Ford was saying. The sound of the sirens blotted out all noise and the crackle of flames singed at Jimmy's arms.

Using his hands, Ford mimicked a man piggypacking a child. Jimmy nodded and dropped on all fours.

Ford backed up and took a running start. He propelled himself off the skinny youth's back as he reached out to the second-floor window ledge. His hands were wrapped carefully within the jacket, but he still felt the intense heat emanating from the concrete.

Nervously, Ford yanked himself up and rapped on the window. After a long few seconds, he saw shadows approach the window.

The frightened façade of Wu Chiong appeared at the windowsill. The old man seemed to be laboring in his breathing. He was struggling with the window frame.

The wood was gathering up intense heat, and the old man's yellowed gnarly hands kept slipping as he clutched vainly at the frame. It was evident he wasn't strong enough to lift the window.

Ford could barely see past the man. The room was filled with thick dark smoke. The only light was from the fiery glow of the fire from the first floor. The ceiling was probably burning. Wu would fall through shortly.

The old man simply shook his head in resignation. He didn't seem scared or sorrowful. He appeared content in knowing he had tried his best to escape. Ford could have sworn he heard the elderly man mutter good-bye.

Angry, Ford gripped the window sill with one hand and then swung himself up. It was an effort to propel his two hundred pound body sideways, but somehow he had achieved his goal. Ford hugged the window, his feet hanging over the short ledge.

He motioned for Wu Chiong to move away from the window, but the old man didn't respond. He had disappeared! Ford prayed that the floor had not given away.

Summoning all his strength, Ford swung a covered hand at the glass above the lock. It shattered inward, splintering shards all over the room.

A gust of smoke choked the hero's lungs immediately. He tried vainly to call out for Chiong, but his throat didn't cooperate.

He peered inside. He spotted the purple robed man lying on the floor. Flames now licked at the office doorway. Soon the place would be engulfed.

Ford twisted the window lock. The metal seared at his fingers as he pulled back in shock. Gritting his teeth, he made a second attempt. Ignoring the burning pain, he found a grip on the lock and freed it. The window sprung upward.

Somehow Ford wedged his massive frame through the tiny opening and was able to drop inside the office. He heard the floorboards groan and creek. One foot slipped through the buckling wood. He felt himself lurch forward. He knew if he fell, the momentum would cause the floor to crash inward.

With a spectacular effort, he twisted his body until he was on firm footing. All the time, smoke gripped his lungs, eager to snuff the life out of him.

Ford tugged at the old man's body. There was no response. He couldn't be sure the old man still lived, but he continued his effort. The flames were weakening his system, he felt woozy as he tried to lift the frail man.

Even the tiny body of Wu Chiong proved too much of an effort for Ford. He was only able to drag the man a few inches. He felt his eyebrows singing off. His arms began to itch. He knew time was precious.

With a herculean effort, Ford pulled the unconscious form of Wu Chiong toward the window sill. His efforts were purely instinctual now. The smoke completely blinded him.

He stuck his head out the window, thankful for the brief respite it offered. He knew he would have to act quickly.

Down below, Jimmy McGee and the firefighters had formed a circle. Their faith in Ford Jones was unwavering. They had spread a blanket, a dozen men gripping it tightly.

Ford could read the lips of the men below urging him to leap to safety. He ignored their request and gulped one last mouthful of air. Plunging back into the inferno, he put the last of his strength into heaving the old man over the ledge of the window. He was careful not to let Chiong bleed himself on the deadly shards.

The frail Chinaman fell like a rag doll toward the blanket. It reminded Ford of his baseball days with the Detroit Wolves. The blanket resembled a giant catcher's mitt as it swallowed up Chiong's body.

Ford waited for the men to unroll the tiny man from the confines of the blanket so he could jump. His nostrils were assailed with fumes and he could barely stand. For a brief second, he felt flames and saw smoke coming from the rubber souls of his shoes. It was too late; he couldn't wait for the blanket to be unfolded again.

He would rather break his back than burn to death.

Closing his eyes, Ford flung himself over the ledge. The tip of his boots caught the sill causing him to be inverted. He fell face forward to an inevitable death.

In the brief seconds his body traveled through the air, Ford centered his mind on an image of Myra Ellington, content that he might see her in some afterlife.

He waited for the fatal contact of the sidewalk to greet him. Instead, his body jolted on impact with a haphazardly spread blanket. The momentum carried him and his saviors into the street. Ford couldn't feel a thing. He tried to talk. A sudden fear of paralysis overwhelmed him.

• • •

Ford awoke to find Jimmy McGee standing over him. The stench of Jimmy's breath suggested he hadn't brushed or rinsed in a long time. Ford waved an arm for him to step back.

"Well, either I'm alive or this is the big guy's cruel idea of hell!" he whispered hoarsely.

Jimmy McGee stretched back and removed his bowler.

"I'm offended!" he barked, before cracking a huge grin. "I knew you'd snap out of it, you stubborn block of stone!"

Ford winced at the sound of Jimmy's screech. His vision started to focus and he realized he was in a hospital room.

"Don't worry," said Jimmy, "I made sure they didn't take you to Mercy General."

"Chiong?" Ford stuttered.

Jimmy snorted. "Guy's fireproof. I hear he's been demanding to go home already. That junior wannabe, Denny, is down the hallway now, sucking up to him."

"And the girls?"

Jimmy sighed. "Linda Mae passed out and Myra, well you know how that girl feels about you. She pitched a fit when she saw it was you being carted away on a stretcher. Didn't stop hollering until we reached Bayview. Finally, one of the young docs sedated her. I'll go fetch her.

Ford gripped his friend's arm. "Wait!"

"Yeah?"

"You know that fire was arson?"

Jimmy nodded. "A probable conclusion."

"Can't be a coincidence that someone tries to burn down old man Chiong's temple right after we visit Warren Lee."

"A good point. I'll ask him."

"What?"

Jimmy reached for his bowler. "Yeah you heard right. He's here, at Bayview. I understand he was distraught and decided to pay his respects to Chiong."

"Must have caught a private boat?"

Jimmy shook his head. "Nope. He was already in Oakland. Some folks had spotted his traveling circus making the rounds earlier tonight."

"Another coincidence?"

"Good question!"

The voice emanated from the doorway. Wu Chiong's right-hand man, Denny, stood under the door frame. His immaculate shoes were covered in soot and streaks of grease stained his forehead. His fists were clenched tightly.

"How is Wu Chiong?" Ford asked with genuine concern.

"Angry, as am I." Denny proclaimed. He entered the room and made a show of closing the door.

Jimmy watched him cautiously.

"Easy, now…" the Irishman suggested.

Denny caught his apprehension.

"Merely wishing to maintain our privacy, Mr. McGee. The Nine Blades honors the sanctuary of a hospital, but I fear my rivals may not."

Ford tried to sit up. The pressure on his hands stung. One hand was heavily bandaged.

"You will bear a scar for your efforts," Denny noted.

Ford ignored the comment.

"Jimmy said Warren Lee was in town, before the fire."

"And after." Denny finished. "Apparently, word reached him of our concerns, and he had decided to confront Wu Chiong personally."

"Confront is a strong term." Jimmy intervened.

Denny gave him a prudent stare.

"However you wish to define the moment, the facts are evident. Warren Lee has built an ever-expanding empire across the Bay. For months now he has tried to broker a deal between the San Francisco clans and our humble members of the Nine Blades. Each time he has met resistance. I believe tonight marked the end of his patience."

Ford forced himself to sit up. A wave of nausea slapped him in the face. He swallowed a mouthful of his own bile.

"Strong accusations, Denny."

"But with cause," Jimmy ventured.

Denny darted eyes back and forth between the two private investigators.

"Wu Chiong trusted you men."

"As well as he trusted you," Ford countered.

Denny grew angry.

"The old tiger appeared vulnerable, but he merely represents an image of the Nine Blades. The entire clan itself will grow even more powerful now."

"With you as its leader?" Jimmy spoke out loud.

Denny relaxed. "And why not? A true leader cannot appear weak when vipers such as Warren Lee lay in wait."

"You're forgetting one thing," Ford offered. "Old man Chiong ain't dead yet."

"And for that we are eternally grateful," Denny responded.

A rapping on the door interrupted their conversation as a commotion could be heard in the corridor. Female voices entwined in verbal sparring.

Jimmy McGee guffawed.

"You know who just woke up!"

Myra Ellington shoved open the door, nearly knocking Denny over. Her face was wrought with fear, and the bags under her eyes hung heavy. She ignored Denny completely and headed over to Jimmy McGee.

She slapped him in the face as hard as she could.

"What gives doll?" the Irishman protested, rubbing a palm against the welt.

The beautiful songbird stared at him defiantly.

"You let them knock me out!" She slapped him again.

Jimmy scampered over to the corner like a school boy serving detention. It was only then, that Ford allowed himself to speak.

"I'm fine Myra."

Myra Ellington sauntered up to his bedside, huge tears streaming down her cheeks. At that moment, Ford loved her like never before.

He didn't see the hand coming as it slapped across his face.

"Say what?"

"You will bear a scar for your efforts."

"Ford Jones! Don't you ever scare me like that ever again!" She pounded a weakened fist against his massive pectorals. "They said you stopped breathing for half a minute!"

"Okay! Okay! So my heart works now. Stop punching it."

Myra hadn't realized she was still hammering away at his torso. She began to laugh, weakly at first but then hysterically. Jimmy almost whimpered.

"You big idiot!" she roared. "I thought I lost you!"

Ford forced himself to hug her. The pain in his burnt hands evaporated, at least for the moment.

"You know you can't get rid of me that easy." He mumbled.

Jimmy's bravery grew brighter. "That's right toots. I need the big guy to be my best man."

Myra wiped the tears from her eyes. She choked back her nasal cavity.

"Then you better stop that nasty drinking, you silly little leprechaun!"

Jimmy burst out laughing, the tension having disappeared from the room. That wasn't the only thing that had left. Denny had slipped out without notice.

"I'll give you two some privacy." He explained. The couple weren't listening. Ford had locked lips with Myra in a deep embrace. He gave Jimmy a thumbs up.

Jimmy McGee left the room in search of his girlfriend. He crossed paths with Warren Lee in the hallway. The handsome Asian simply nodded at him. Another figure was entering the elevator. Jimmy couldn't tell who it was Warren had been conversing with. Instead his eyes focused on the darkened footprints the man had left behind.

• • •

Ford Jones was a man of little patience. He considered a hospital stay to be detrimental to his business.

"Can't earn if I'm couped up," he had complained.

Myra Ellington was all too pleased with his decision. She didn't trust doctors, specifically white ones. Her experiences had proven distasteful, she had explained. Ford didn't probe. He knew the girl had his best intentions in mind.

Jimmy McGee filled out the paperwork and tried to pay the bill. Much to his surprise, the tab had been picked up by Warren Lee. Jimmy decided it prudent to withhold this information from Ford.

The muscular investigator refused to leave until he paid his respects to Wu Chiong. Jimmy knew it was better not to argue. He marveled as Ford dressed himself and departed the sterile room, Myra in tow.

Denny stood outside Wu Chiong's hospital room, an unlit cigarette flittering back and forth between his nervous fingers. He eyed Jimmy McGee suspiciously.

"Couldn't afford the luxury suite?" the Chinaman teased.

Frustrated, Jimmy pushed past the tired man. He was immediately met with resistance by two scar-faced members of the Nine Blades Clan.

"Just want to visit the old skin bag," Jimmy protested.

Denny had recovered his dignity. He smoothed back his oil slicked hair. "Wu Chiong will only see his savior. His words not mine."

Ford grunted and sidled past the ugly goons, careful not to let his wounded palms touch the door. He whistled sharply as he encountered the shocking image of Wu Chiong breathing through an oxygen tube.

The wrinkled man waved a claw-like hand and beckoned Ford over to his bedside.

"You don't look too comfortable," Ford joked.

With a sizable effort, Wu Chiong removed his breathing apparatus. He managed a weak smile, his yellow fangs flashing briefly.

"I imagine this bed is a tad more comfortable than a casket."

Ford grinned and pulled up a chair. He sat close enough to the old man so the others couldn't hear their conversation.

Jimmy and Denny were too entrenched in a death stare competition to notice. The brutes knew Ford could be trusted. They were enjoying the antics of Denny and the tiny Irishman.

Wu Chiong pointed at a glass of water with a straw in it. Ford quickly held it to the old man's mouth.

"You do know the fire was set?" Ford asked, already knowing the answer.

Chiong swallowed the mouthful and nodded. "It was deliberate. Whoever set it was familiar with my schedule. They knew my men patrolled the restaurant all evening long. The only time those doors don't have eyes on them is during the final shift change."

Ford took comfort with the fact that Chiong was sharing vital knowledge with him.

"Is that how they were able to chain the door?"

"Undoubtedly."

Ford pondered, "Warren Lee was in Oakland tonight."

The elder Chinese man nodded his head.

Ford continued, "Do you think he was behind this?"

"He will, assuredly, have an alibi. I did not ask him when he came to visit me."

"What did you talk about?"

Just then, Denny re-entered the hospital room, evidently bored with his staring contest. He quickly pulled up a chair on the other side of the bed.

"Wu Chiong needs his rest."

Ford agreed. The old man looked parched.

"Forgive my associate." Chiong blurbed. "He has the impulses of a child and the recklessness of an elephant."

Denny razzed his leader in disgust.

"Wu Chiong is angry that I assumed temporary command while he was under the doctor's care."

Chiong's eyes flared.

"Command? You were making decisions without my consent!"

Denny bowed. "Forgive me exulted one. I could not appear weak in the face of our rival."

"You're talking about slick Warren Lee?" Ford begged.

Denny continued to twirl the cigarette in his fingers. He stared intently at the old man.

"Our headquarters is ruined. Our reputation is soiled!"

Chiong forced himself from the bed, the effort causing him to choke. Ford quickly offered the glass of water, much to Denny's dismay.

"The building can be rebuilt," Ford stated.

Chiong grinned dementedly.

"What?" Ford offered.

Denny answered, "Warren Lee offered to buy out our interests. He promised a staggering amount of money."

Chiong intervened. "In return, the Nine Blades would fall under his control."

Ford waited for Denny to respond. The young Chinaman stood up and paced around the hospital room.

"Denny?"

The youth only looked at his leader. His words were intended for him.

"Perhaps that wouldn't be a bad thing."

Ford remained silent. So did the elder Chinaman.

Denny continued, "We have grown old and stunted under the old system. Our elders age stubbornly while the youths continue to have their ideas and proposal shot down. As a result, Oakland has not prospered the way San Francisco's Chinatown has blossomed."

"By cutting in the white man in our business?" Chiong spat out venomously.

"Why not?" Denny countered. "Look at what Lee has done across the bay. Some say he is responsible for that bridge being built."

"Then why isn't he being honored this weekend?" Chiong fired back.

Denny shook his head in amusement. "Honor? Glory? These are the things that drive the elders. What has it gotten you, Wu Chiong? A string of broken down storefronts? Washing the white man's dirty underwear? Where is the honor in that vile task?"

Chiong glared at his number one man.

"You have profited greatly from those businesses, Denny. You own more property than I ever did at your age. I don't see the failure in that."

Ford remained silent, apprehensive to interrupt the feud.

"Listen to this fool!" Denny proclaimed. "Warren Lee offered us a partnership, Wu Chiong. We could have rebuilt with his money. No more stupid laundry-mats or chopstick take-outs. We could have broken ground on night clubs, casinos, high-end stores!"

"Under Warren Lee's control," the old man finished.

"That's right honorable one, because he has set an example. His rollout has worked magnificently in San Francisco and it would have worked here."

"Would have?" Ford mumbled out loud.

"I declined," Chiong explained. "Patience is a virtue my young pupil must learn. To enter a deal with the devil who brought hellfire to our doorstep would be unwise."

Ford agreed with the old man, but he kept his opinion to himself.

Frustrated, Denny threw his arms up in the air.

"You are not needed here, young one." Chiong stated. "You would be wise to remain visible among our clan. Let the Nine Blades know our future is strong."

This seemed to calm down Denny somewhat.

"What would you have me do?"

Chiong pondered for awhile. "Right now your waterfront business becomes our most valuable asset. Set up headquarters there. Make a show of it, as many foot soldiers as you can muster."

Denny nodded. "And your restaurant?"

"My father built that temple brick by brick and we will do the same. It will rise like a phoenix, I promise. We will rebuild a bigger, better restaurant. Put aside any notion of Americanized night clubs. The people of Chinatown need the familiarity that my restaurant emanates." He paused long enough for Denny to let it soak in. "You will honor my wishes?"

Denny hesitated, but only for a second.

"Of course, the Nine Blades will rise stronger!"

Much to Ford's surprise, the youth rushed out the door without saying goodbye. Old Wu Chiong seemed satisfied with the encounter. Ford was still shocked that he was allowed to witness it.

"Mr. Jones, you will, of course, disregard anything you may have overheard in this room. The business of the Nine Blades does not concern you."

"Of course."

Only Ford didn't believe his own words. His mind kept replaying a vision of the fabulous buildings Jimmy and he had encountered across the bay, all legally funded and open to everyone. Maybe Denny was right? Maybe Wu Chiong's vision of Chinatown was outdated? Had Warren Lee grown so impatient with progress that he ventured to force the old man's hand?

Ford wondered as Jimmy finally fought his way past the unpleasant visages of Wu Chiong's men.

"Howdy, wrinkles!" he offered. "Never thought I'd say this, but you seem attractive compared to those soldiers you got guarding the room."

Chiong forced a grin, "Mr. McGee, you never disappoint me. Just when I wonder if my refusal for integration is wrong, you show up to confirm my opinion."

"Well, uh, glad I could help you out," Jimmy sputtered.

Ford laughed out loud. "That was an insult, Jimmy."

The Irishman feigned depression, "You stab at me, Chiong!" He turned to his partner. "I think we have kept our dates out long enough, my good man."

Ford nodded, carefully lifting himself from the chair. He placed a gentle hand on Wu Chiong. "Get well old man."

Chiong patted his arm.

"I will not forget what you did."

Jimmy winked at the frail Chinaman. "Next time I see you, I expect a fresh batch of fortune cookies."

Chiong smiled.

"Better hold on to that woman, Mr. McGee. She has yet to sample my more exotic potions."

Jimmy raised an eyebrow.

"So I take it I will be on the guest list when you re-open the rathole?"

"Unless you intend to propose somewhere else?"

Jimmy was shocked. "How did you? Never mind, I know, ancient Chinese secret and all that."

Wu Chiong tried his best to wink back at Jimmy, but his eyelid refused to cooperate. He merely squinted instead.

"There's a rude insult on the tip of my tongue," Jimmy teased. "But you have suffered enough for one day. I'll send in the big uglies now."

He departed, racing to catch up with Rutherford Jones. The big man was way ahead of him, eager to get out of the confines of the hospital.

"Wait up Ford! I want to make sure your girlfriend doesn't take another swing at me!"

Ford didn't hear him. He was too deeply involved, churning the words Denny had spoken over and over:

"We have grown old and stunted under the old system."

*   *   *

The next several days were spent cheerfully upgrading the office. Ford and Jimmy had settled on adding an inexpensive sofa to their mundane workspace. After a brief debate, they had agreed to rotate sleeping arrangements. Each man would get to enjoy bunking down on the sofa three nights at a time while the other was stuck with a cot. Ford would go first due to his injuries.

Myra remained extremely busy. The demand for entertainers had skyrocketed during the days leading up to the Bay Bridge opening. Many of the architects and engineers were staying in Oakland, eager to make that first car trip to San Francisco. This had resulted in overflow crowds at the local hotspots. Owners were desperate to keep the clientele. Myra was hired under the condition that Rutherford Jones did not attend any of her shows.

A definite buzz was in the air. Herbert Hoover, himself, was scheduled to cut the ribbon, signaling the beginning of a new era in California transportation.

At least once a day, Jimmy or Ford strolled down to Chinatown to check on the progress being made in repairing the neighborhood. The burned out shell of Wu Chiong's old business had been leveled, an empty lot filling its vacancy.

Ford was amazed at how quickly the debris had been removed. The pride and efficiency of the local Chinese folks could not be matched. No trace of the burning rubble could be detected. If not for the torched sidewalks, all evidence of the calamity had been erased.

Wu Chiong, himself, had returned to the neighborhood, reluctant to relocate to his waterfront holdings. He knew those facilities were in capable hands with Denny. The fiery youth had calmed down in the moments after the attack, focusing his energy on expanding his stronghold on the pier. New money had managed to work its way into town, and Denny was determined to mine it for all it was worth.

There had been no further sightings of Warren Lee. The affable businessman had accepted Chiong's rebuke and returned home to prepare for the bridge opening. He did, however, manage to recruit all of the restaurant and laundry workers who had been displaced by the ravenous inferno.

Chiong had given his personnel his blessing to work for Warren Lee. What else could he do? They had to sustain themselves, and many were disgusted at the thought of joining Denny's illegal wharf racketeering. No, Chiong preferred these good and honorable people take their skills across the bay.

He had confidence they would return once his empire was rebuilt. Denny shed no tears at the loss of these employees. What good would chefs and cleaners be in a world of violence? The truth was, he was overjoyed of ridding himself of the elderly and frail cooks who Chiong insisted on keeping despite their slow pace and sloppy habits.

Denny had plans on recruiting new thugs to his side of the bay.

Back at the jewelry shop, Linda Mae had begun an inventory clearance. Her goal was to free up space in order for Jimmy McGee to move in. The only problem was, Jimmy wasn't informed of the plan. The skinny youth had grown chilly to the idea of marriage.

"Can you imagine how Oakland will change when the bridge opens?" Linda Mae piped up optimistically. She was polishing a worn display case.

Jimmy looked up from his newspaper.

"How so, babe?"

The tired looking blonde continued to rub at the glass with a rag. She wasn't making much progress. She probably wouldn't. The case was decades old and had hundreds of scratches across its surface. Still, this didn't deter her from giving it an old elbow rub.

"The big wallets from Frisco can drive over the bridge without having to worry about getting mugged on the boat or something."

Jimmy frowned. "What makes you think they would want to travel here, to Oakland?"

Linda Mae smiled, "It's cheaper here."

"It's cheaper because it's less desirable. Listen, honey, don't fall for all that spiel the big wigs are spewing. The folks over in Frisco are a different sort. They don't want to come here, and they sure as all hell don't want us to go there."

"James McGee, you watch that cursing!"

He shrugged. "Just calling it how I see it. Sides, that toll will scare most people away."

"The toll is a necessary inconvenience," Linda Mae explained. "The government spent seventy-five million dollars on that project and if you ask me, it's very reasonable for them to request a surcharge for the upkeep of the bridge."

Jimmy folded the paper in frustration.

"I'm sick and tired of hearing about the Bay Bridge. It's going to be a headache, darling. Mark my words. Oakland will never be the same."

"I certainly hope not." She spit, very un-lady like on the glass and rubbed harder. "Do you think Rufus and Myra will copy us?"

Jimmy rolled his eyes. "Say again?"

"Marriage? You know, monkey see, monkey do!"

Jimmy shook his head in amazement. "Poor choice of words, my love."

Linda Mae was oblivious to his comment.

Jimmy elaborated. "Who knows? They're grownups. It's not impossible."

Linda Mae finally gave up the battle. She tossed the soiled rag aside and wiped a small bead of perspiration from her brow. For the first time, Jimmy noticed a hint of gray at her temples.

"Listen, doll, I know I said I want to marry you, and I do, but let's not rush into things."

A stunned look of pain developed on her face.

"Jimmy?"

"Oh don't give me that look, baby. You know I love you. It's just that the business is still taking baby steps, and speaking of babies…"

Linda Mae was still. Her eyes welled up.

Jimmy could tell he had hit a raw nerve.

"You did it again, McGee." He cursed at himself.

"No, Jimmy, I understand, really I do. A young man like yourself. You're not ready to settle down. You still want to sow your oats. Is that what they call it these days?"

Jimmy bolted out of his chair, embracing her stiff form.

"It ain't like that at all, doll. I only have eyes for you."

He wiped away a tear that had escaped the corner of her eye. Embarrassed, Linda Mae turned her back on him. Jimmy gripped her about the waist and hugged her tightly.

"I'm just a little scared Linda Mae."

She could feel the honesty in his voice.

"Me too, Jimmy, but if I stopped every time I was afraid of something…"

Jimmy McGee kissed the back of her neck gently. He breathed in the sweet aroma of her perfume intermingled with the sweat she had worked up. His eyes closed, as he whispered.

"You're the best thing that ever happened to this guy."

She swung her hips around to face him, her eyes red from sobbing.

"I'll wait for you, Mr. McGee."

He kissed her gently on the lips. She closed her eyes and smiled. A chill ran down Jimmy's spine. Anxiety kicked in. He relieved the tension by breaking the embrace and grabbing a broomstick.

"What's this?" Linda Mae questioned.

Jimmy swept the floor briskly.

"Just doing my part, my lady. Maybe, you're right. Maybe the president is right. This black cloud hanging over America might just be lifting."

• • •

It turned out that Jimmy McGee was wrong about the Bay Bridge. Anticipation for the grand opening was at a fever pitch. Every available member of law enforcement was being deployed to San Francisco.

The bridge wasn't even open yet and it had caused a gridlock.

Rutherford Jones slammed down his phone receiver. He had just ended a brief conversation with Wu Chiong.

"Damn peculiar!" the giant growled.

Jimmy McGee glanced up from his newspaper. It seemed every page was filled with descriptions and accounts of the activities scheduled for the ribbon cutting ceremony.

"Boring rag!" He fussed. "You know if smart people really wanted to make a buck, they'd fill these pages with information about movies and music and anything except for the same tired old news."

"It's called a newspaper, Jimmy."

The skinny youth nodded his head in agreement. "So what got your gander up, boss?"

Ford crossed his arms, biceps bulging against his shirt.

"Wu Chiong told me he received a report from the pier that Warren Lee had arrived in Oakland on a private charter."

Jimmy raised an eyebrow.

"On the eve of the bridge opening? He'll never make it back in time."

"You think old man Chiong is being paranoid?"

Jimmy shook his head. "Chiong has been playing his part for too long to have a miscue."

"If that's so, what could possibly be so important that Warren Lee would miss the biggest spotlight of his life to slum down to Oakland?"

All the color drained from Jimmy McGee's face.

"Unfinished business!"

Ford bolted from his chair. He hesitated, before deciding not to take his gun. With his hand bandaged he didn't feel comfortable trusting his aim.

"Grab your jacket, Jimmy. I have a hunch Chiong might need our help."

"But you promised the girls we'd watch the fireworks from the waterfront!"

Ford zipped up his windbreaker. "I never said we wouldn't. But it might be a good idea to check on Chiong's interests at the pier."

Jimmy let out a sigh.

"We might run into Denny, and he ain't too friendly these days."

Ford agreed. "Wonder why that is?"

Jimmy grabbed his lucky bowler and locked up the office.

"You know the women will want to freshen up."

Ford shook his head. "No time. I'll grab the car. You come up with some excuse for them to meet us down by the waterfront."

Jimmy's eyes bulged out.

"Me? I get to be the bearer of bad news? Oh brother!"

Ford gave him a stern look. "Chiong sounded nervous."

"I'd be nervous too if I snubbed a kingpin like Warren Lee. But do you really think he'd try something tonight?"

"Makes sense."

"How so?"

Ford explained. "If things get out of control, the entire Oakland PD is across the bay on patrol. It will be open season for criminals."

The last bit of color washed from Jimmy as his knees wobbled.

"The perfect time to finish Wu Chiong off and Warren Lee has come down to do it himself!"

•　•　•

Jimmy had fed the girlfriends a weak tale of business woes which much to his relief they swallowed wholeheartedly. Nothing could diminish their excitement over the evening's festivities and to be honest, they cherished the extra time to get ready.

Both women felt as if it was a holiday, and in a sense it was. Businesses had closed down early to allow employees to make plans for the evening. The sidewalks were already filled with patrons eager for the celebration to begin.

Ford had driven down to the pier where huge containers were being unloaded from barges. Denny and his men had taken advantage of the lax security to increase their smuggling operation tenfold. They knew harbor security would not have the time for a thorough search of each vessel.

Satisfied that nothing was being disrupted, Ford and Jimmy made the short drive to Chinatown and searched out a parking spot. Business was brisk. Many thrill seekers had ventured down to partake in the inexpensive food while waiting for the fireworks to begin.

"Shame old man Chiong's palace was burned down. He would have cleaned up tonight!"

Ford ignored his friend. His eyes were focused on the unruly crowd that had gathered at the arch of Chinatown.

"Seems like a lot of folks got a head start on drinking," he mused aloud.

Jimmy concurred. The mob scene was noisy and a bit unsettling. The lack of law enforcement was very troublesome.

"What was the commissioner thinking when he ordered all his men to head over to San Francisco?" he barked over the hum of the crowd.

Ford muscled his way past the revelers.

"Simple. It's a matter of importance. Herbert Hoover and Hollywood's elite versus thousands of lowly foot traffic. Who do you think the government is going to protect?"

Jimmy was knocked sideways by a shoulder from a heavy set man. The gent continued on without noticing.

"Damn Ford! Maybe it ain't safe for the girls to be down here tonight!"

Ford's eyes drifted over the crowd of excited party goers all jockeying for prime viewing space of the fireworks which were still several hours off. Many of the folks were intoxicated. Some were just rowdy men blowing off steam.

"If Warren Lee is going to make a move, it will be tough to keep everyone out of harm's way."

Jimmy nodded, jostling through the crowd. Their destination was a local charm store that Wu Chiong had set up shop in. During his brief conversation with Ford, Chiong had mentioned the owners would be closing early for the evening.

Ford saw a group of revelers harassing a pair of pretty young Chinese girls. The girls were barely out of their teens and despite their protests, were being wolf-whistled by a horde of frat boys intent on a good time.

"I know what you're thinking, big guy, but we don't have time." Jimmy protested.

The chant of the impulsive men grew louder.

"What if that were Linda Mae and Myra? How would you feel if someone just let that happen to them?"

Jimmy sighed, knowing the argument was already lost. "Okay, just go scare them off and be on our way."

Ford stalked over to the group. By this time, the two girls cowered back to back, slapping away groping hands.

There were hordes of people around the group, but no one bothered to intervene. Ford pushed his way through the rubbernecks craning to see some action. Without a word, he grabbed one of the ruffians by the collar and lifted him off his feet.

"Black bastard!" the youth growled.

Ford responded by dropping him to the pavement...hard.

"One warning," he announced. "That's all I'll give."

His expectations were met when two of the drunken antagonists moved forward. Ford wasted no time reacting. His fist shot out, striking the first one on the jaw. The drunken frat member would wake up with some loose teeth tomorrow.

Undeterred, the boy's friend advanced forward. That was a mistake. Ford caught him in a bear hug, inhaling the stench of stale beer as the youth belched. He stared at Ford with crossed eyes.

"Why you ni..."

He wasn't able to complete the slur. Ford head butted him across the eyebrows, ripping open a patch of skin and causing a splurt of blood to trickle down the inebriated man's forehead.

"Any of you other goons stupid enough to try your luck?" Jimmy McGee asked.

The remaining members of the group shrank back as they caught the glow of Ford's face in the moonlight. He was a raging bull, ready to dispense a beatdown on any who crossed his path. The youths quickly sobered up and scampered off, not bothering to help their fallen comrades.

Jimmy McGee handed the blood-drenched youth a handkerchief.

"Clean yourself up, kid." He watched as the thug stumbled away. "And show some respect for women."

The other youth that Ford had slammed to the sidewalk crawled away on all fours, his pride forgotten as he raced for the safety of the shadows. Ford gave him a playful boot on the seat of his pants to aid his progress.

The two Asian girls were still whimpering when Ford turned to face them.

"Don't hurt us!" they begged. The younger of the pair sought comfort behind Jimmy McGee.

Unmoved, Rutherford Jones unclenched his balled up fists and stalked off in the direction of Wu Chiong's charm shop.

Jimmy McGee attempted a clumsy bow at the two girls, but that only increased their sobbing. Frustrated, he waved an arm at them and trotted off after his partner.

The night had gotten off to a rough start.

• • •

The noise level began to increase along with the size of the crowd. The harbor was overflowing with all types of vessels, everything from gigantic yachts to homemade rafts all battling for precious real estate. Many of the larger boats were blaring their horns in anticipation of the unveiling.

Ford and Jimmy had given up hope on finding the girls. They knew Myra was street smart and would keep an eye out for the boisterous Linda Mae. Right now the crowd was shoulder to shoulder. Jimmy wondered if the entire country had shown up.

"Big guy I'm starting to get claustrophobic!" Jimmy announced, weaving his way around a pack of youngsters who were climbing up light poles for a better view.

Ford nudged his way closer to the sidewalk. He could spot the quaint charm shop Wu Chiong had sheltered in. The lights were on but the shades were drawn. The surrounding storefronts were mobbed with visitors, most just eager to escape the crush of the maddening throng.

"Jimmy, follow me."

Determined, Jimmy McGee put his head down and bulled his way forward. He was within a few feet of his partner when he felt a draft. Someone had swiped his bowler!

"Oh no, you don't!"

The Irishman reached back, grabbing the collar of the thief. His fingers tried to form a grip on the shredded material, but the shifty youth was too quick for him. Jimmy watched as the boy disappeared, swallowed up in the sea of revelers.

"Stop fooling around McGee!" Ford ordered.

Frustrated, Jimmy took one last look at the crowd, searching in vain for his lucky bowler. Reluctantly, he gave up the chase and maneuvered over to Ford. The big man had managed to clear a space around himself with some not to subtle elbows.

"Damn, Ford! I didn't sign up for this."

"Quiet, Jimmy." Rutherford Jones hammered on the door of the charm shop. His massive fists almost smashed the glass windows.

"Maybe, he can't hear you," Jimmy offered.

Ford tried to peer through the blinds. He could make out shadows moving swiftly throughout the shop.

"Someone is inside."

"Probably too scared to open the door," Jimmy guessed.

Ford studied the building.

"I'm going around back. You stay here and keep pounding on the door."

Jimmy mumbled something incoherently, but Ford was already gone, his powerful legs propelling him past the frenzied mob.

"Open the door or I'll smash the glass!" Jimmy threatened.

He hadn't expected a response. He was shocked when the door swept open. A well-tailored arm reached out, and before he could react, Jimmy McGee was yanked through the doorway.

"Whoa nelly!" he barked, stumbling across the floor.

The door slammed shut behind him. He heard a bolt being latched into place. Sprawled on the ground, Jimmy raised his eyes to behold his captor.

"You!"

The well-tailored man was Warren Lee. The usually confident businessman was frazzled. His shirt was torn in front and his hair was tousled. He gazed at Jimmy, but couldn't speak.

"What gives? Where is Wu Chiong?" Jimmy demanded.

He found the answer huddled in the corner of the dimly lit shop. Chiong was attired in his favorite purple robe, his knees drawn up to his chest and his head hung low. His breathing was labored.

"You scumbag!" Jimmy McGee barked at Warren Lee.

Lee didn't move. A manic expression flashed across his face as swung his head around the room.

Jimmy McGee attacked before the man could locate a weapon. He hurled his thin form at the Chinese entrepreneur with great gusto. The momentum hurled both men in the direction of the frail Wu Chiong who was unable to get out of the way. They bowled into him with tremendous force, knocking the old man into unconsciousness.

Warren Lee finally found his voice.

"Stop! You've got it all wrong!"

Jimmy wouldn't buy any of it. He continued his assault, pummeling the man with a series of windmill punches. Lee tried vainly to block the blows, but most of them landed brutally.

Sensing victory was imminent, Jimmy McGee increased his fury. He continued to hammer his opponent until the man grew weak. With one final uppercut, Jimmy felled him.

Wiping his bloody knuckles upon his pants leg, Jimmy McGee congratulated his feat. He heard a polite clapping behind him. He turned, expecting to see his partner, Ford Jones. Instead, it was Chiong's protégé, Denny.

"Well done, McGee!" He continued to clap, smiling with insane glee.

Jimmy was sucking in oxygen, trying to catch his breath.

"I saved him," the skinny Irishman proclaimed.

Denny erupted with laughter.

Confusion splashed across Jimmy's face.

"Am I missing something here?"

The handsome Asian reached inside his topcoat. When his hand emerged, a snub-nosed revolver occupied it.

Jimmy felt the euphoria dwindle from his body.

"I messed up," he whispered.

Denny couldn't contain his elation. "Bottles, Bottles, Bottles! Always playing second fiddle, like me. Difference is I did something about it." He waved the gun in the direction of his unconscious employer. "Old man Chiong continued to spew his tired old rhetoric about the old ways, and I begged him to listen."

He kicked the bleeding form of Warren Lee.

"So you're the cause of this mess?" Jimmy accused.

Denny bowed. "Warren was just a rube. He's a smart cookie. Made bundles revitalizing San Francisco, and he offered us a chance to do the same thing here in Oakland, but stubborn old Chiong wouldn't listen to his offers." Denny's eyes bulged with fury as he continued his explanation. "I burned down the restaurant, thinking the old man would finally give in and accept the offer, but I underestimated his stubbornness. The old crone insisted on rebuilding his vision of a tired old Chinatown filled with noodle joints and laundry mats."

Jimmy was listening, but also wondering where Ford was. The big man should have made his entrance minutes ago.

"Oh, you're wondering where muscle brain is?" Denny read his mind. "Funny thing about the heroic types. I kind of expected him to come in the back way so I sprung a trap. The very best warriors of the Nine Blades were waiting back there for him. I have a feeling your act will be solo from now on."

Jimmy let out some air. "So what was Lee doing here tonight?"

Denny grinned even wider. "I lied. I told him old man Chiong had come to his senses and accepted the deal. I was going to kill Chiong and frame Warren Lee for the murder. Only problem is you started banging on my door before I could finish them off."

Jimmy calculated his chances. Denny was a few feet away and a proven menace. With Ford out of the picture, Jimmy was the only one standing in the way.

"I know what you're thinking, McGee, but don't try it. Your friend is gone and old man Chiong isn't worth it. Nothing has to change between us. We can still keep our old alliance going. In fact, you'll make more money."

Jimmy forced a weak grin. "You really did lose your marbles. Lee was right about one thing. Law enforcement is winning the war on crime, and your old ways will be a thing of the past." He kneeled down and felt Warren Lee's pulse. "He's still alive. So is Chiong. You can still stop this insanity, Denny."

Denny's grin transformed into a malicious scowl. "No! No longer will I be subjected to this tyrant. It's my turn to run things!"

He raised the gun toward Jimmy.

The skinny Irishman closed his eyes; his only thoughts were of the friends he would leave behind.

"Just get it over with," McGee pleaded.

Unmoved, Denny aimed the weapon and prepared to squeeze the trigger, but before he could fire, old man Chiong sprung forward like a cobra, his purple robe enveloping the pair. They tumbled to the ground. There was a brief struggle and then the gun went off.

The roar of the boisterous crowd nearly blocked out the sound, but Jimmy McGee still winced as the blast deafened him. He flinched as the robe settled and then was tossed aside.

Denny stood up, a shocked look on his face. He pointed the gun at Jimmy, who cowered in the corner, awaiting the fatal bullet.

It never happened.

Denny toppled over, his mid-section soaked with blood. The bullet had struck him in the abdomen.

The gun clattered across the floor as Jimmy McGee dove for it. He clutched it wildly, holding his breath, his eyes darting back and forth.

"Get up you idiot!"

It was Wu Chiong barking at him. The old man stood naked except for a pair of boxer shorts. His purple robe lay on the ground.

Jimmy stared in wonderment at his wrinkled savior, before bursting into a joyous whooping. He hugged Chiong with genuine affection, but the old Chinaman shoved him away.

"Get back, moron! Are you trying to break my back?"

Jimmy couldn't answer him. He was too happy at the turn of events. His shouting had startled Warren Lee out of his stupor.

Lee wiped the blood from his chin and looked down at his torn clothing.

"I don't remember what happened!" he proclaimed, stumbling around the room.

Jimmy McGee cleared his throat.

"Denny attacked you."

Chiong nodded, looking ridiculous in his underwear.

"McGee is correct. Denny administered a ferocious assault on the two of us. We are fortunate, Mr. McGee arrived when he did."

Warren Lee tried to shake the cobwebs from his skull.

"I feel like someone is shooting cannons off in my head."

A hulking shadow entered the storefront.

"The sound you hear is the fireworks," the newcomer announced. "The Bay Bridge is officially open for business."

Jimmy stared up. A wide grin enveloped his face.

"Ford! You're alive!"

Rutherford Jones winked at his partner. "Sorry I was late for the party. I ran into a roadblock." He flashed his balled up fists, the skin torn from battle. He stared down at the lifeless body of Denny. "Looks like you handled things okay in my absence."

Jimmy's mouth dropped open. "Well, actually…"

Old man Chiong interrupted him. "McGee was like a viper. Denny never stood a chance."

Ford raised an eyebrow.

Jimmy shrugged. "You taught me well, boss." He shielded Ford from his view as he gave the venerable Chinaman a thumbs-up.

The men were quiet, the clamoring sounds of music and fireworks filling the air.

"The party started without us," Ford said nonchalantly.

Jimmy's smile evaporated. "The girls!"

Ford bit his lower lip, "They will not be happy."

Wu Chiong had retrieved his purple robe. He tied the sash around his waist in an effort to restore his dignity.

"I think my friend here might be able to help us."

Warren Lee nodded, feeling his skull for bruises.

"Yeah, I have a private boat and the harbor patrol will escort us back to San Francisco. I think your dates might enjoy a few days at one of my properties."

Jimmy wrinkled his nose. "But we didn't pack any clothes."

Ford slapped him on the back. "If all goes right, Jimmy McGee, you might not need any!"

THE END

ABOUT OUR CREATORS

AUTHOR -

ROBERT RICCI - is the author of Blood on the Cobblestones. He graduated from Curry College, class of 1986 and is a lifelong resident of New England who grew up on a steady diet of Doc Savage novels, classic comic strips like Terry and the Pirates, etc. He loves the classic heroes, Flash Gordon, Tarzan, Conan and all the rest. He's also a huge fan of 1960s television series. Last but not least, he's the proud father of two adult young ladies and lives a quiet life with his better half, Dorothy.

INTERIOR ILLUSTRATOR -

ANDREW RITCHIE - is a second shift freelance illustrator and a first shift corporate graphic designer. After receiving his BFA from the University of Wisconsin-Eau Claire, he illustrated work for role-playing games and comic books for over 20 years. He was born and in raised in western Wisconsin where he still lives with his wife and two daughters. More examples of his work can be found at http://andrew-ritchie.tumblr.com/

COVER ARTIST -

PAT CARBAJAL - started as a political cartoonist at various national newspapers in Argentina. Since then, he has illustrated a wide variety of impressive projects, such as Adamant Entertainment's TALES OF FU MAN CHU and FOE FACTORY: MODERN , TIMELINE OF THE PLANET OF THE APES by Rich Handley. Pat's illustrations for ROCK AND ROLL COMICS: THE SIXTIES featured Ozzy Osborne, AC/DC and Guns n' Roses. Pat's first full-length graphic novel as the sole illustrator was ALLAN QUATERMAIN, published by Bluewater. For the comic series VINCENT PRICE PRESENTS, Pat debuted as a writer as well as illustrator. Other works include the upcoming JAMES BOND LEXICON for Hasslein Books. Pat also creates exclusive T-shirt designs for Rotten Cotton Graphics.

GANGSTERS & GUNMOLLS

It was the 1930s and America was locked in the grip of the Great Depression. Gangsters controlled the major cities while outlaws roamed the rural back country . It was a time of Speak Easy gin-joints, Tommy-guns, fast cars and even faster dames. This is the world of New York based Private Investigator Rick Ruby, a world he is all too familiar with. From the back alleys of Gotham to the gold laden boulevards of Hollywood, Ruby is the shamus with a nose for trouble and an insatiable appetite for justice. So if you've got a taste for hot lead and knuckle sandwiches, tug your cuffs, adjust your fedora and light up a Lucky, a brand new pulp detective is coming your way. Created by pulp masters, Bobby Nash & Sean Taylor, Rick Ruby echoes the tales of Sam Spade and Philip Marlowe while offering up his own brand of two-fisted action. Joined by fellow pulp smiths Andrew Salmon & William Patrick Maynard, these modern scribes of purple prose present a quartet of tales to delight any true lover of private eye fiction.

Every Story a GEM!

THE RUBY FILES

Introducing
RICK RUBY
Private Eye

PULP FICTION FOR A NEW GENERATION!

AN AIRSHIP 27 PRODUCTION

NEW PULP

AVAILABILITY:
AIRSHIP27HANGAR.COM

Making Pulp History!

From the heart of Africa to the streets of Harlem, a new hero is born sworn to support and protect Americans of all races and creeds; he is Damballa and he strikes from the shadows. When the reigning black heavy weight boxing champion of the world agrees to defend his crown against a German fighter representing Hitler's Nazi regime, the ring becomes the stage for a greater political contest. The Nazis' agenda is to humble the American champion and prove the superiority of their pure-blood Aryan heritage. To achieve this end, they employ an unscrupulous scientist capable of transforming their warrior into a superhuman killing machine.

Can the mysterious Damballa unravel their insidious plot before it is too late to save a brave and noble man? Airship 27 Productions and Cornerstone Book Publishers are proud to introduce pulpdom's first ever 1930s African-American pulp hero as created by the acclaimed author, Charles Saunders.

"Having revolutionized the genre of epic fantasy with the creation of Imaro, a black warrior easily equal to such classic characters as Tarzan and Conan, Charles Saunders has done it again. This time he has created DAMBALLA, a true hero in every sense of the word. Battling racism and evil in the 1930's, DAMBALLA is no pale imitation of The Shadow or The Avenger. In fact, after reading this excellent book, I think that they would be proud to consider him a brother in the ceaseless war against crime and injustice." – Derrick Ferguson -- "Dillon and the Voice of Odin"

AIRSHIP27HANGAR.COM

New **PULP**

PULP FICTION FOR A NEW GENERATION!

For availability: Airship27hangar.com in PDF format

BASS REEVES
FRONTIER MARSHAL

BASS REEVES
FRONTIER MARSHAL
VOLUME ONE

ANDREW SALMON · DERRICK FERGUSON
GARY PHILLIPS · MEL ODOM

FROM AIRSHIP 27

A WESTERN LEGEND COMES TO LIFE
FEATURING RIP-ROARING, WILD-WEST STORIES BY:
GARY PHILLIPS, MEL ODOM,
ANDREW SALMON
& DERRICK FERGUSON

PULP FICTION FOR A NEW GENERATION!
FOR AVAILABILITY: AIRSHIP27HANGAR.COM

AN AIRSHIP 27 PRODUCTION

www.ingramcontent.com/pod-product-compliance
Lightning Source LLC
Chambersburg PA
CBHW071241250626
47163CB00001B/275